PRAISE FOR THE MIGHTY MUSKRATS MYSTERY SERIES

THE CASE OF WINDY LAKE, BOOK ONE

"The Muskrats feel like the kind of real kids that have been missing in children's books for quite some time."

—QUILL & QUIRE

"Chickadee's rez-tech savvy pairs well with her cousin Otter's bushcraft skills, and, along with Atim's brawn and brother Samuel's leadership, the four make a fine team. …an Indigenous version of the Hardy Boys full of rez humor."

—KIRKUS REVIEWS

"[A] smart and thought-provoking mystery for middle grade readers."

—FOREWORD REVIEWS

THE CASE OF THE MISSING AUNTIE, BOOK TWO

"Missing Auntie is a good read, with an emotional punch, and I can hardly wait for the Mighty Muskrats to take their next case."

—JEAN MENDOZA, AMERICAN INDIANS
IN CHILDREN'S LITERATURE (AICL)

"A compelling 'urban bush' adventure that offers light and reconciliation to dark truths."

—KIRKUS REVIEWS

"[D]elivered a surprising end to the story, one that left me envious of the close family ties Chickadee and the boys enjoy."

—THE MONTREAL GAZETTE

THE CASE OF THE RIGGED RACE

≪≪ A MIGHTY MUSKRATS MYSTERY ⋙
BOOK FOUR

THE CASE OF THE RIGGED RACE

MICHAEL HUTCHINSON

Second Story Press

Library and Archives Canada Cataloguing in Publication

Title: The case of the rigged race / Michael Hutchinson.
Names: Hutchinson, Michael, 1971- author.
Series: Hutchinson, Michael, 1971- Mighty Muskrats mystery ; 4.
Description: Series statement: A Mighty Muskrats mystery ; book four
Identifiers: Canadiana (print) 20220193193 | Canadiana (ebook)
    20220193207 | ISBN 9781772602890 (hardcover) | ISBN
    9781772602210 (softcover) | ISBN 9781772602227 (EPUB)
Classification: LCC PS8615.U827 C368 2022 | DDC jC813/.6—dc23

Edited by Kathryn Cole

Printed and bound in Canada

*Second Story Press gratefully acknowledges the support of the Ontario Arts
Council and the Canada Council for the Arts for our publishing program.
We acknowledge the financial support of the Government of Canada
through the Canada Book Fund.*

Published by
Second Story Press
20 Maud Street, Suite 401
Toronto, Ontario, Canada
M5V 2M5

www.secondstorypress.ca

This book is dedicated to the teachers who had to put up with me in the past, including Mr. Penner, my Grade 5 teacher. Much respect to those who inspire a desire to learn and give their students the tools they need to educate themselves. Hats off to all the teachers that rise to the challenges presented by their students. My apologies to those teachers that were there with me as I went through my crazy years. Much thanks also to those Elders and First Nation teachers who have shared their knowledge with me as I continued my learning journey into adulthood. There is always more to learn.

- M. H.

CHAPTER 1

Dog Down!

"Where is he?! All the other sled racers are in, and Atim is still out there!"

Looking down the snowy trail, Chickadee's brown, freckled face held a worried frown as she squeezed her cousin Otter's arm.

The smallest and most bush-wise of the Mighty Muskrats, Otter put a comforting arm around Chickadee's shoulders, but his voice betrayed his own concern. "There's so many things that can go wrong for a musher, but you can't just assume it's the worst."

Chickadee rolled her eyes at him as she gathered her long, black hair and tossed it over her shoulder. "Yeah, but the worst is a possibility too, right? We have to get a snowmobile and go look for him."

The Windy Lake Trappers Festival was in full swing. People from all over the province's North, and a few dozen from farther away, had come to celebrate the trapper lifestyle and its gifts to a newborn Canada. The week and weekends were filled with social gatherings, educational events, and competitions of skills needed for the fur-trade industry and pulling a living out of the bush. The overall winners of these contests were crowned the King and Queen Trappers of the North for the year to come, and those bragging rights would last a lifetime.

The Muskrats had always been inseparable, and they had been given the name Mighty Muskrats by their oldest uncle, who had watched them laugh, fight, poke, and snap at each other as they grew up. The nickname had spread across the First Nation and each of their exploits added to the Mighty Muskrats' reputation.

Atim, the tallest and most physical of the sleuths, had taken their older cousin's dog team out on the teen race and had been expected to place, solely on the experience of the dogs. But the team and its Muskrat musher had still not arrived long after all the other sleds crossed the finish line.

Samuel, Atim's little brother and the Muskrats' bookworm, shaded his eyes against the glare of blowing snow. His short, cropped hair stuck out from under his toque, and his thin frame was wrapped in a dark blue snowsuit. The cold, blustery day added to the worry about his missing brother. He looked around to see if he could speak to any of the race volunteers—hopefully someone with a walkie-talkie had some information.

Otter smiled reassuringly at his cousins, but he was a lot more familiar with the wide range of things that could go wrong when five excited dogs were tied to a sled. "Atim is a new musher. He may have Jody's team, but that doesn't mean things are going to go off without a hitch. Hey, Jody?"

Their older cousin nodded and laughed. "Totally, Otter. Don't get too worried." From his wheelchair, Jody gave Samuel a playful shove. "It's not easy controlling a dog team. Atim's pretty good, and my team is great, but this is their first race together."

Samuel snickered. "Says the guy whose dogs broke his leg!"

Jody's eyes narrowed. He was sitting in a wheelchair, a thick parka keeping his top half warm, his bottom half covered in a blanket. A plaster-bound leg protruded ahead of him, propped up by a shelf attached to the chair. After feigning anger for a second, Jody's brown face broke into a smile. "Listen, it was my dumbness that got me hurt. My dogs were doing what they were supposed to do—running. Not their fault if their musher couldn't keep up!"

"Hard for you to keep up when you're kissing trees." Otter punched his older cousin, affectionately.

Jody laughed. "Tapwe. True. Trees are *not* good kissers...."

The roar of a snowmobile pulling up on the other side of the fence that separated the spectators from the race ended the conversation. While the boys were talking, Chickadee had borrowed a snow machine, towing a sled, from their uncle. "Get on, you Muskrats. Let's go find Atim."

Otter looked at Jody. With a nod, he offered to stay with him.

Jody gave him a push. "I'll be here when you get back, Otter. Someone will bring me hot chocolate." He watched the boys jump the fence from his wheelchair that sat on two toboggans, married together with plastic crazy carpets tacked along their bottoms. "I'd be crazy to get pulled behind a snowmobile that Chickadee was driving in something as flimsy as this."

Chickadee rolled her eyes at him. "Do you mean your old body, cousin?" She gunned the engine.

The boys held on as if their lives depended on it.

The Windy Lake First Nation was on the shores of the huge lake that gave the community its name. Although the First Nation made up the bulk of the neighborhoods, the Métis and Canadian communities just off the reserve were starting to grow. The houses and neighborhoods of Windy Lake were scattered amidst evergreens and outcroppings of ancient limestone. Back in the 1950s, a pit mine had opened up near the community. A generating station and dam had been built on a nearby river to provide electricity to the facilities.

The Trappers Festival and its many events attracted

people throughout the area. The Windy Lake Teen Dogsled Race was a warm-up for the organizers, volunteers, medics, and veterinarians before the final event that was the Windy Lake International. Hundreds of people were involved in the adult dogsled race, but the teen race the week before gave the main managers and head volunteers some experience starting teams, running checkpoints, taking care of injured or hurt mushers and dogs, and wrapping up at the end. Of course, the adult race was many, many miles longer—from Windy Lake to Smokey Bend and back. But the teen race was still full of competition, sweat, teeth, and tears. As they left the finish line of the race, the Muskrats had no idea where along the way they would find Atim.

Chickadee drove all vehicles like she was made of steel, seemingly unconcerned that she, or her passengers, felt the effects of gravity and momentum, had nerve endings, or would carry a collage of bruises the next day. Due to her concern for Atim, she was driving more crazily than usual.

Otter and Sam bounced helplessly within the sled. Otter was in its basket, with Samuel trying to hold on to the handlebars. Two bumps and an S-turn later, Samuel was lying on his back in the sled, his legs pointed at the sky, as Otter bounced along the trail trying to get his feet onto the back of the sled's skis.

After twenty minutes of reckless careening down the trail, the snowmobile rumbled to a stop.

The last big bump on the trail had violently slapped the boys together into the basket of the sled. Otter pushed Samuel off and into the snow beside them. Sitting up, he looked around.

They were in the middle of the bush. An unremarkable stretch of the race route among the thin trunks of tightly packed evergreen trees. With their bottom branches shed to give more resources to those closest to the warmth of the sun, the trees were a stand of skinny, steel-gray pillars.

"Atim!" Chickadee yelled. Startled, Otter and Sam leapt to a standing position.

The largest of the Muskrats was walking toward them, tears in his eyes. In his arms, he held Jody's lead dog, a big, black Husky mutt named Muskwa. The dog's head rolled sideways, and its long tongue hung from the side of its mouth. Atim fell to his knees, openly sobbing. He laid the dog on the snow.

Chickadee ran to her cousin, slid to his side, and threw her arms around him. "What happened?!"

Atim covered his face in gloved hands, his shaggy hair falling over them, then he slapped his ski pants. "I don't know! We were going so well. Then Muskwa started heaving, hunching over, like he was tossing his cookies as he ran." With a mitted wrist, Atim wiped a tear from his eye. "He slowed down, took us off the trail, and then back, like he was staggering. Then he stopped and fell over."

All the Mighty Muskrats were now kneeling in the snow around the listless dog.

Samuel put his hand on Muskwa's rib cage. "He's still warm. I think he's breathing."

Otter petted the dog. "Yeah, it's like he's sleeping!"

Muskwa took in a big breath and exhaled a sigh. The Muskrats all shared relieved looks, their teardrops changing from drips of worry to tears of relief.

Samuel looked past his brother at the race volunteer wrestling with the other four dogs from Jody's team.

The volunteer had arrived by snowmobile moments before the Muskrats and was now losing a raucous battle with the other sled-pullers. Still in their harnesses, the big canines were obviously worried about their leader. In a mad frenzy, they tangled themselves and the volunteer in a hopeless mess.

"I think that guy needs help." Samuel lip-pointed at the volunteer, wrapped in four different canine personalities all doing their own thing.

Otter began to walk over. Sam followed.

A tear fell from Atim's eye and then slipped between the slick black hairs of the shallow-breathing dog. "Muskwa's a good dog."

Chickadee nodded and put a hand on her cousin's shoulder.

The dog let out a wheezy snore. The two cousins smiled at each other.

Chickadee smirked. "Kind of lazy, don't you think? Taking a nap in the middle of a race?"

Just then, Sam returned. "I brought the dog bag. We better get him bagged up and to the vet as soon as we can."

"Good idea!" Atim nodded at his younger brother and took the bag.

With care, the three Muskrats spread the canvas bag on the snow, opened it, and slowly slid it up Muskwa's body, gently folding the dog's limbs, so they could tighten the drawstring at his neck.

Chickadee spoke to Muskwa as they worked. "Easy, boy, this will be a bit uncomfortable, but it will keep your legs and paws safe while you're traveling in the sled."

Otter patted Muskwa's large head, once it was all that was sticking out of the canvas sack. "Good dog. Now you won't be able to jump out of the sled while it's moving."

Atim gently lifted the lead dog and carried him to the borrowed snowmobile. He laid Muskwa carefully on the floor of the sled and then got in behind him, holding the dog's head on his lap.

Atim looked up at Chickadee, who was already straddling the snowmobile. "Go slow?" Atim looked at his cousin with pleading eyes.

Chickadee nodded sincerely.

Sam shouted over the bubbling of the snowmobile engine, "Otter and I will make sure the rest of the dogs get back!"

The volunteer and Otter, the most bush-wise of the Muskrats, had untangled and gained control of the team and were maintaining order by keeping the lines, dogs, and sled stretched between them. The team seemed to be cooperating.

Chickadee slowly did a U-turn, threading between the thin evergreen trunks and back onto the trail. With a wave they took off more slowly than when they had arrived.

"I hope Muskwa will be okay," Otter said as they watched the snowmobile head down the trail.

The volunteer started his engine. "You'll be fine with taking the dogs back?"

Otter nodded and smiled. He pulled his mitts on, held tightly to the sled's handlebar, and yelled, "Hike! Hike!"

The four dogs lunged, putting their shoulders against their harnesses, and the sled shot forward.

Sam hopped onto the back of the volunteer's sled, and they followed Otter down the trail.

Back at the race's endpoint, they could see Atim and Chickadee hurrying the bagged dog into the veterinarian's tent.

As the snowmobile rumbled to a stop, Samuel was surprised to hear angry yelling. Looking around, he spotted a group of agitated protestors leaning over the fence and gesturing toward his cousins.

The mob was in a frenzy! With fingers pointed, they screamed, "Dog killers! Dog killers!"

CHAPTER 2
Animal Army

"What was that all about?" Chickadee was wide-eyed as she helped Atim carry the big dog.

Atim looked rattled. "If I hadn't been so worried about Muskwa, I would have been more freaked out."

The two Muskrats were surprised to see the volunteer veterinarian was their favorite teacher, Mr. Penner, who was wearing a white medical coat and big snow boots rimmed in gray fur. They *galunked* quickly, as he walked toward them.

The Trappers Festival needed so much effort and so many resources that whole families were involved in one way or another. Rather than fight the flow, the school gave the students the week to explore and learn more about their community and the fur-trade culture that added the Canadian and Métis neighborhoods.

"What happened? Is he breathing?" Mr. Penner's hair was the color of coffee with a touch of cream. Above a ready smile, his mustache looked like two comfortable caterpillars. The reason the Muskrats listed Mr. Penner as their favorite teacher was because he always spoke to them as equals. He never spoke down to them or treated their feelings as if they were less valid than his own. As he was also a volunteer paramedic and firefighter, his role as a stand-in dog doctor wasn't too big a stretch.

Mr. Penner gently took Muskwa from the Muskrats and placed him on the table. The sound of the protestors outside increased a bit as Samuel and Otter stepped into the tent.

"Ho-leh! Those people are upset about something." Sam shook his head as he scanned the room.

Mr. Penner and Atim carefully removed the sled dog from the canvas bag. Muskwa was dead asleep. He flopped weakly out of the bag.

The volunteer vet looked over the rim of his glasses at the new arrivals. "Those are members of the Animal Army. They've taken a disliking to the sled dog race this year."

"Why?" popped out of Sam's mouth before he could stop it.

Mr. Penner rolled Muskwa onto his belly.

As Mr. Penner checked the big dog's eyes, ears, nose, and throat he absentmindedly mumbled, "I'm sure they'll tell you if you ask them." He continued to examine

Muskwa, moving around the table to be closer to different bits.

After a few moments of further examination, the vet shrugged. "You know, besides the fact that he's asleep, there doesn't seem to be anything wrong with this dog."

Atim was serious and sincere. "He sure seemed sick when we were on the trail and now he won't wake up. Has he been poisoned?"

Mr. Penner went to a metal cabinet along the tent wall and pulled a plastic packet out of a drawer. "What did you see?"

Atim thought back. "Well, we were going so smooth, and maybe that was why it was so obvious when he started doing something weird. Every now again he would hunch over. I didn't know what he was doing, but when he got sick later, I thought maybe he'd been heaving. You know, throwing up."

"Vomiting? During the race? Hmm…. He looks like an experienced dog. This isn't his first race?"

The Muskrats all shook their heads.

Otter's brow was furrowed with concern. "He's our cousin Jody's dog. Muskwa has run a lot, pulled a lot of sleds. Races at least two or three times a year."

Mr. Penner opened the packet and pulled out a small needle. "I'm going to take some blood. We have to check all the dogs that place for possible stimulants. Sometimes people use drugs to make their dogs run faster. I'll take some of his blood and see if there is anything in it that shouldn't be there."

"Thank you, Mr. Penner." Sam bobbed his head in appreciation.

"The results will take a while. He isn't foaming at the mouth and his breathing is regular. It doesn't seem like poison, but I would like to keep him overnight for observation."

The young investigators watched as the vet lifted one of Muskwa's forelegs and inserted the needle.

The Muskrats all squinted one eye as they watched the needle go into his skin. A dozing Muskwa let out a little whimper as Mr. Penner drew out some blood.

Once he had his sample, Mr. Penner patted Muskwa. "If he had eaten something that wasn't good before the race, it may have had an impact as he ran. The stomach needs a lot of blood. May account for his grogginess after getting sick." The doctor pulled off his rubber gloves, threw them away, and leaned against the metal cabinet. He looked at Atim. "Do you remember where you were on the trail when he started hunching over?"

Atim flicked the hair out of his eyes and pursed his lips. "I...think so."

Mr. Penner smiled at the cousins. "Sounds weird, but if you could find his vomit, we might be able to figure out if he ate something that made him sick."

Otter giggled. "You want us to go on puke patrol?"

They all chuckled.

Mr. Penner, still smiling, nodded. "Yeah. I guess so. Find out what his stomach couldn't deal with, and maybe we'll discover what led to his loss of energy."

Looking down at the dog, Mr. Penner told them he would be sure to keep an eye on him and would call in a real vet if it looked like Muskwa was getting sicker. "Here's my e-mail. Send me a note in the morning and I'll let you know how Muskwa is doing and if you can pick him up."

After the Muskrats said good-bye, the vet lifted the tent flap for them to leave. The protestors' chants met them, along with a blast of cold air. Mr. Penner shrugged. "You'll have to get past them." He looked at the Muskrats, encouragingly.

Atim scowled. "What's their problem?"

Mr. Penner looked over his shoulders at the activists. "Hmm…. I can only speak in general, but I would guess a lot of them are young people from the city. Probably lived all their lives getting their meat on a nice little Styrofoam tray. Lived their whole lives, up to recently, with no idea what went into getting that boneless chicken breast onto their table. They want to make the world a better place—a world without pain or blood or mess."

"Are they coming from a good place?" Samuel pinched his chin.

"In most cases, yes, coming from a good place, but

maybe a wrong perspective." Mr. Penner smoothed his mustache with the hand that was not holding the tent flap. "For me, I grew up on a farm, so we always had animals we could name. But then, we had animals my parents didn't allow us to name because they would be food one day. We also had working animals—horses to haul wood out of the bush. It's why I felt comfortable to do a couple of shifts as a vet for the teen race. I'll just be an assistant for the adult race."

"Why are they so angry about it?" Otter sounded concerned.

"They believe what they are doing is right, I guess. And they believe in their perspective…enough to scream about it." The Muskrats' teacher shook his head. "Don't let them scare you. Race security has them pretty corralled in that area. I'm sure they'll let you through." He motioned for the Muskrats to step through the tent flap.

With a few good-byes, the four investigators left the tent and went to look for where their Uncle Jacob was taking care of the rest of the dog team. When the protestors saw them, they ramped up their venting.

"Dogs are not our slaves! Free your dog! Free your dog!"

Sam shaded his eyes against the glare of the sun on snow to look back at the protestors. "I'm glad they're on the other side of the fence. They look rabid."

Chickadee was scouting their path ahead and suddenly

broke into a jog. "There's Uncle Jacob and Jody. Looks like they got the other dogs loaded."

The Muskrats ran over to where their uncle was loading Jody's wheelchair and toboggans into a trailer that already held the dogsled. Jody was in the passenger's seat of their truck. In the back of the vehicle, was a wooden structure that looked like a stack of windowed boxes. It was big enough to allow the individual dogs inside to curl up comfortably, but small enough that they would not be hurt sliding around with the motion of the vehicle. The noses of Uncle Jacob's other dogs could be seen in the little, round windows.

Uncle Jacob wore a checkered lumberjack jacket, and a pair of canvas work pants that were stained with everything from animal blood to car oil. His graying, black hair was shaggy, and it was obvious he had skipped a few visits to the barber. His ancient toque, slightly too small, perched at an odd angle on his round head suggesting it was about to fall off, but it never did.

Making his living out of the bush in the summer, Uncle Jacob smelled like fish from pulling nets on Windy Lake. Now that it was winter, he smelled slightly of carnage; the blood, fur, and fluids of the animals he trapped and skinned. The Muskrats often wondered if Uncle Jacob was impervious to cold, heat, swamps, snow, mosquitoes, and hunger. The only thing that seemed to annoy him was people who talked too much.

Jody was his son and main helper, but now that Otter was older, the smallest Muskrat had spent the past few summers working with them both, helping them tend and train the dog teams.

Jody leaned through the open passenger window and watched the Muskrats approach with a serious look on his face. He lip-pointed at Atim. "Where's Muskwa?"

Atim's shoulders drooped. "I'm so sorry, Jody. He was perfectly fine at the start of the race, but he…like, passed out while he was running. We took him to the vet tent. He's still sleepy now, but other than that he seems fine. He is staying there for the night, just in case there is something seriously wrong with him."

Jody hit the side of the truck angrily. The thump carried across the race grounds. "I told you to take care of my dogs!"

Atim stammered, "Jody! I did look after him, and I got him to the vet tent as soon as I could. Mr. Penner will watch him, and we can call in the morning."

"A teacher! What does he know? I've had Muskwa since he was a puppy. I told you to take care of him, especially!" Jody was obviously distraught.

"I *did* look after him. It wasn't my fault!" Atim's voice rose in frustration.

Up to this point, Uncle Jacob had been listening but hadn't said anything. Now, he leaned forward, his voice low. "Now, boys…."

Atim and his older cousin looked at the ground. They both gave their heads a shake.

The tallest Muskrat looked at his injured cousin in the truck. His brow furrowed angrily as he spoke. "Do you want me to keep in touch with the volunteer vet, or do you want to do it?"

Jody paused before he spoke. "Just bring me back my dog!"

In the silence that followed, the Muskrats' uncle nodded his chin toward Chickadee. "You can bring my snowmobile back tomorrow." Then he turned slightly to tease his niece. "Make sure you bring it back in one piece."

Chickadee laughed, and dramatically rolled her eyes. "I will, Uncle. I'll take it easy on the boys."

Their uncle turned and walked to the driver's side of the truck. Once inside, Uncle Jacob, always trying to use laughter as a way to smooth things over, smiled at Atim. "Hey, don't worry about not finishing your first race. Jody didn't finish his first one either."

Atim cringed, but then smiled. "Thanks, Uncle. It isn't easy controlling five dogs, but I think, with a little more practice, I'll cross that finish line next year."

"That's the attitude. Just because you're a big loser today, doesn't mean you'll be a big loser tomorrow."

Atim's jaw dropped. The other Muskrats burst into giggles.

"Ever jarred!" Otter slapped Atim on the shoulder.

Jody laughed as his father drove off.

Suddenly, Samuel smacked the legs of his ski pants. "Ahh, poop!"

Chickadee raised an eyebrow at her cousin. "What's up, Sam?"

Samuel threw up his hands. "I forgot to ask Uncle Jacob what he thought of the protestors."

Otter shrugged. "You'll get your chance. I doubt the Animal Army traveled all those hours to Windy Lake just for the teen race. The big show is the adult race at the end of the week."

"You're right. If they want to be disruptive, for sure that's what they'll be aiming for," Sam said thoughtfully and nodded in agreement.

Atim was listening but was obviously agitated. "Right now, I want to figure out what made Muskwa sick. Will you help me, Otter? You're the best tracker out of all of us. We have to find that puke."

Otter laughed. "That's a sentence you don't hear too often. Let's go out there first thing in the morning!"

CHAPTER 3

Lab Gab

When the trees beside the trail seemed to match the memory of Muskwa's first heaving, Atim tapped Chickadee on the shoulder, and Uncle Jacob's snowmobile rumbled to a stop. The light of a new day was dimming as a flood of clouds poured over the sky. The branches of the trees made the racetrack darker still.

Leaping off the snowmobile, Atim looked back at his little brother, Sam, and cousin Otter. The two were still holding on to the sled, their looks of desperation slowly giving way to the realization they had come to a full stop.

Atim chuckled. "Smooth ride?"

Chickadee had already jumped off the snowmobile, picked a direction, and was walking away scanning the trail. She yelled over her shoulder, "Maybe too dark to see anything! You sure this is the right place?"

Atim was helping Sam and Otter out of the sled. "I

think it is the right place. There was a long stretch of trees and then, I saw that place where people could watch. I figure he started heaving just before or just after that. But who would be watching the race way out here?" Atim pointed to an area where the race organizers had made a spot for spectators to collect.

"We're close to the Cedar Point turnoff. The highway is just down there a little ways." Sam pointed to a thin bush road that led off into the woods behind the spectators' area. "There's a few families that live down there, and there's the staff and guests from the hotel, restaurant, and gas station."

Chickadee, cold and impatient, slapped her hands against her arms. "We better hurry up! It's freezing. Atim, let's go this way and check. You two, go that way."

Otter started walking in the opposite direction and Samuel followed him, rubbing a bruise earned during the challenging ride.

The smallest of the Muskrats had been orphaned by a car accident at an early age. He had been raised by their grandfather and late grandmother, which made him the most bush-skilled of the four young sleuths.

Sam knew that once Otter got into tracking, there was no point in talking to him. He was quiet at the best of times, but when his nose was on the trail, he was in hunter mode—quiet and stealthy. The voices of Chickadee and Atim filtered through the trees. They were speculating what color Muskwa's puke would be, as they searched in the other direction.

"Not a lot of light down here. Hard to see." Otter spoke more to himself than Sam.

Sam kicked at some snow. "I hope we're in the right place. Who knows if Atim picked the right spot."

"Well, there are not too many of these audience places, so if he remembered that, there's a good chance this is the place."

"Hmm." Sam looked up, bored, his head hanging back, his mouth open. He followed Otter.

Otter was bent over, his face within a foot of the ground. "Hey! Check this out."

Sam came forward. There in the snow was a round clump of…something.

"Touch it." Sam gave Otter a little nudge.

"*You* touch it!" Otter pushed him back a little harder.

Sam made sure his mitt was on tight, then reach out and quickly touched it. "Whatever it is, it's frozen…hard."

He picked it up. The two boys studied it in the dim light.

"Looks like a meatball." Otter pushed on the lumpy, reddish-pink orb in his cousin's hand.

"I think it is." He offered it to Otter. "Sniff it."

Otter pushed it back. "*You* sniff it."

Sam lifted it to his nose. "It's frozen. Doesn't smell like nothing."

Otter smirked. "Maybe it's your nose that's frozen."

Sam giggled and tried to wiggle his nose. "Could be."

He looked in the direction that Chickadee and Atim had disappeared and yelled, "Heeyyy, you guuyysss! I think we got something."

In a moment, they could hear the heavy footfalls of running snow boots. Chickadee was slightly short of breath after the jog. "What...did you...find?"

Atim grabbed the clue from his brother. "Looks like a meatball." He showed it to Chickadee.

Otter shrugged. "That's what I said. I found it over there." He lip-pointed.

Atim's face was conflicted. "You know, if Muskwa was trying to grab one of these while he was running...it could look like he was heaving."

Samuel was pinching his chin. "You ever see Jody throw meat at the dogs? Muskwa is always the quickest."

The rest of the Muskrats agreed.

"But it's just a lump. What does it mean?" Atim scratched his head beneath his toque.

Sam shrugged. "Could be nothing."

With his greater knowledge of the bush, sled dogs, and racing, Otter speculated. "It could be bait dropped by some trapper. It could be something someone in the crowd brought for lunch. Maybe a dog treat that fell off a racer's sled."

Atim blinked and nodded. "But what if it *is* something?"

Sam considered the idea for a moment. "We found it around the audience area. It could have been thrown on the trail on purpose. Maybe in the hope of slowing down the racers." He shrugged a shoulder. "But right now, it means nothing."

Chickadee nodded, but her brow furrowed in thought. "If we find another one, it would be less likely to have been dropped by accident, wouldn't you think?"

Sam raised his eyebrows at the thought. "Not sure, but let's look around. If it is a clue, the more we have, the better. Right?"

Atim pointed in the direction that he had scoped out with Chickadee. "We've checked out the area in front of the audience. Let's all go this way." He indicated they continue past the viewing spot. The four young detectives spread out along the trail.

The Muskrats soon found three more of the frozen orbs. However, farther from the spectators' area, there was nothing to be found in the churned snow of the racetrack.

Out from his pocket, Atim pulled a selection of Ziploc bags. After shuffling through them, he chose the second largest. "Let's put them all in here."

Chickadee looked at Atim, her eyebrows quizzical.

He shrugged. "There's a lot of free food when the Trappers Festival is on. You never know when you can stock up. I always carry plastic bags, just in case."

The other young detectives laughed as Otter dumped the balls of meat into the bag.

★

"There he is!" Atim yelled as he walked across the parking lot of the Windy Lake School.

Mr. Penner was trying his best to hold on to the leash of an ecstatic Muskwa. The big dog lunged against the leather strap, pulling their teacher forward a step or two. "He's certainly wide awake now."

The Muskrats' favorite teacher had e-mailed them and told them to come pick up Muskwa at the school.

The Windy Lake School was one of the biggest buildings on the reserve. Empty of students for the week, the school housed numerous festival events, meetings, and seminars within its battered walls.

Chickadee squinted against the sun as she looked up. "Mr. Penner, can we use the science lab and a microscope?"

"Of course! As long as you respect the equipment. You must have found something." Mr. Penner led them back into the school. Atim was now wrestling with the big black dog as they walked through the halls. Once inside the science lab, Mr. Penner gestured to a bowl of dog food and a bowl of water that sat in the corner of the room. "Tie Muskwa to that handle there by the food."

Otter helped his cousin tie up the big dog.

It was obvious that Mr. Penner had been sorting through his outdoor winter gear, getting ready for another volunteer shift with the festival. He lifted the gear off the table at the front of the room and took it into the back room. When he returned, his big mustache couldn't hide the curiosity in his smile. "Okay. What have you got?"

Samuel held up the bag of the thawing balls of meat. "We got to take a look at this stuff before it starts to stink."

"Can I see?" Mr. Penner pushed his glasses up his nose and sat as Sam handed the baggie over.

Their teacher swiveled on his stool to examine the Muskrats' clue. "Looks like meatballs. How are these important?"

Atim smirked. "We've been asked to find out if they're Swedish or Italian."

Sam laughed, smacked his brother's arm, and chimed in, "I think he means Swedish or American. In my opinion, they're too small to be Chinese."

Chickadee shook her head at her cousins, "Sheesh. You're both meatballs. Sorry, Mr. Penner."

The teacher smiled and shook the Ziploc bag. "They're certainly a recipe for droll jokes, apparently."

Otter chuckled but kept on track. "We found them on the race trail. We don't know if they're important or not. But we think they may be what made Muskwa sick."

The teacher took another look through the plastic bag.

"You think there may be something in them?"

Samuel had taken the microscope from its shelf and brought it over to the lab table. He gave a few glass slides to Otter. "We don't know. But like Chickadee always says, we can't make bannock without flour. We need more info before we can figure out if these are really a clue."

The teacher nodded and put the bag down. "Well, I trust you'll be careful with the equipment. I'll go tidy up in the back while you do your thing. Let me know if you figure anything out. After you've taken a look, I'll bag up some of this myself and send it to the lab for testing." With a smile over his shoulder, Mr. Penner left the Muskrats to get down to their investigation.

Atim picked up the bag, opened it, stuck his nose in, and took a big whiff. He gagged and dropped the bag on the table. "I…I…think it's gone bad!" He put a clenched hand to his mouth but continued to gag.

Chickadee ran to the end of the table, placing a hand over her nose. "I'm not smelling that."

Otter shook his head and grabbed the bag. "You should smell what the inside of a moose is like." He reached in and pulled out one of the rounded chunks of meat. "Almost all of this is still red, but there are a few browning bits."

Atim looked off into the distance with watery eyes, trying to feel out whether or not his stomach had stopped its convulsions. "I'm never going to eat hamburger again."

Sam snorted. "I give that about thirty minutes." He took the meatball Otter gave him, broke it in half, and gagged. After a second, he gave them a chagrined smile.

Atim pointed at his brother. "Wah-waahh!" The other Muskrats broke into giggles.

Sam shook his head, grinning. "I can handle it. Just takes some getting used to." He went back to putting some of the meatball onto a slide. He placed another slide on top, and then squished them together. Once he slid them into the clips on the microscope's stage, he gazed through the eyepiece, adjusting the focus knobs. After a moment, he straightened and looked around at his cousins. "I have no idea what I'm looking for."

The three other Muskrats shrugged.

Chickadee laughed. "Us neither."

Sam motioned to the eyepiece, offering it to any of the others.

Otter stepped up. "Well, this isn't wild meat, that's for sure. It's cow."

"How do you know that?" Atim sounded skeptical.

Otter did not take his eye away from the microscope, but he moved the slide over to look at another portion of the meatball. "I knew that while it was still in the bag. I don't know, wild meat is…just different. It looks different, smells different. I think wild animals exercise more than farm ones." After a moment, he pulled back from the eyepiece. "This could take forever. But give me another one."

Sam reached into the bag and pulled out another meatball.

Chickadee held her nose at the end of the table, just in case. "Why don't you look to see if you can find something in the meatballs first? And then, if you find something, put that under the microscope."

"Good idea, Chickadee." Sam dumped the bag of meat on the shiny, washable surface of the lab table.

Atim held his nose but took a sniff from a safe distance. "It's not too bad now."

Otter was digging through the meat with the end of a pencil. "Most of this is still good meat. It wasn't bad hamburger that made Muskwa sick."

Samuel smirked at his brother. "Yeah, and he wasn't dumb enough to stick his nose in a freshly opened bag of it. After it had been sitting for a while."

Atim looked seriously at his brother. "My name is Atim! That's Cree for dog. I live by my nose."

"And your stomach," Chickadee teased.

Otter poked something out of the meat with the pencil and lifted it up to show the group. "Hey, look at this."

The other Muskrats squinted to see what looked like a small bit of yellow-and-white cellophane or plastic.

Sam put the little bit on a slide. "Keep looking in the meat. I'll check this out. See if you can find anything else."

Otter continued to poke through the meat.

A few moments later, Sam pulled his eye away from

the microscope, obviously thoughtful.

"What do you see?" Chickadee asked.

Sam gestured toward the instrument. "Do they look like numbers, or are they just squiggles? I'm not sure if I'm imagining things that aren't there."

Chickadee came around the end of the table, looked through the eyepiece, and focused on the tiny bit. "It looks like a five to me, but it's been scrunched."

"Let me see." Atim approached the microscope, his fear of smelling rotten meat seemingly gone.

"Got another one." Otter held up another little bit, then rubbed it off the pencil and onto a slide. "And there's also a different-colored one." He pulled out another bit of partially dissolved plastic.

By the time each of the Muskrats had a good look at the other bits Otter had pulled from the cow meat, Mr. Penner had returned to see how they were doing. "Find anything?"

Sam stepped back from the microscope, and then lip-pointed toward it. "Take a look, Mr. Penner."

Their teacher studied the clue they had found. After a moment, Chickadee asked quietly, as though to indicate Mr. Penner didn't need to stop what he was looking at to answer, "What do you think it is?"

"Well...." Mr. Penner spoke haltingly as he focused the microscope. "To me, it looks like half of one of the little capsule pills I take before I go for a boat ride." He stood up straight and looked at the Muskrats. "You found more than one?"

Sam replaced the slide in the microscope with one of the others. Mr. Penner studied the new bit and then nodded. "Yes. This one too, it looks like half of a partially dissolved capsule. And I can see without the microscope that final slide has the other half."

Otter picked up the slide and gave it to the teacher, who held it up to the light. "Yep. The other side of the pill."

Sam pinched his chin, thoughtfully. "So, it looks like someone may have mixed something into the hamburger?"

Mr. Penner thought for a second. "Well, best-case scenario, it could be medicine meant for dogs."

Atim screwed up his face, concerned. "What would be the worst-case scenario?"

Sam shook his head. "Worst-case scenario…poison. And someone is trying to mess with the race."

Mr. Penner held up a finger and slid off the stool he had been sitting on. "Give me a moment…."

Their teacher went back into the science lab storeroom. It held all the supplies, equipment, and frog and pig specimens in formaldehyde that would be studied throughout the year.

Otter looked skeptical. "Who would want to fix the teen race?"

Chickadee's brow furrowed. "Almost everyone in the

teen race is from Windy Lake, or one of the towns nearby. It would be terrible if someone was cheating!"

Sam ran his fingers through his short black hair. "You know, we need to figure out what these pills do. Really, this all could still mean nothing. Maybe it is some musher's dog medicine."

Mr. Penner returned from the backroom, he had two yellow-and-white capsules in his hand. "I'm not going to give you these but take a look." He dumped the pills onto the lab table. "What do you think?"

Chickadee leaned close to the pills and then over the fragments. She spoke slowly. "They…look…the same."

Mr. Penner nodded. "An adult can buy this stuff at the drugstore without a prescription. People will even give it to kids for car sickness. Makes them sleepy. You can get it at the Co-op."

Chickadee's eyebrows lifted as she looked at her cousins. "That's something we can check out, I suppose. Do you mind if I take a picture of these?" Chickadee wiggled her phone at Mr. Penner.

The other Muskrats looked up at their teacher, expectantly.

"Go ahead." Mr. Penner adjusted his glasses and gestured toward the meat. "I'll send some of this to the lab for testing."

Chickadee began to take a few pictures of Mr. Penner's pills.

"How long will it take to get the results back from the lab?" Sam asked.

Mr. Penner checked the time. "It's still early. If I send it out this morning, it will be back the day after tomorrow."

The Muskrats' bookworm frowned. "I don't want to wait that long. Do you three?"

The other sleuths shook their heads.

Sam smiled at them and then turned to his teacher. "While you wait for the results, we'll keep poking around."

Mr. Penner scratched his head. "Do you have access to a computer?"

"Well, sort of," Chickadee responded. She was thinking of the old clunker in the Muskrats' fort and wondering if it was up to the task.

Mr. Penner smiled. "You can use the lab if you need to, Chickadee. There are websites that were created to help people learn more about the pills they've been prescribed. There are even sites that will tell you what a pill is, and what it does, just based on a description."

"I'll check those out!" Chickadee sounded excited.

Otter shook his head, his brow rumpled with concern. "I'm still having trouble believing it. It doesn't make sense to rig the teen race, does it?"

Sam considered his cousin's question. "You know, the adult race is in a week. That race is way more important."

"So?" Otter shrugged.

"Well, we're in a science lab, right? Maybe the teen

race was just an experiment."

Chickadee snapped her fingers as Sam's words sank in. "So, maybe someone was using the teen race to see if the drugged meatballs actually worked!"

Sam nodded.

Otter had also caught on. "And…their target is really the adult dogsled race at the end of the week!"

Mr. Penner's eyes grew serious at the thought. "People bet on the adult race. It's part of the North American circuit, and it involves teams and their stakeholders from across the country. You can be sure there will be shenanigans whenever big money is involved."

Samuel snapped his finger and pointed skyward. "It looks like the Muskrats are on the Case of the Rigged Race!!"

CHAPTER 4
Fort-i-fication

"I-I'm g-g-oing to f-f-reeze t-to death!" Atim rubbed his biceps with crossed arms and exaggerated his shivering.

Otter snickered. "Hold on! Our little heater is trying as hard as it can!"

After quietly tying up Muskwa by his doghouse in Uncle Jacob's backyard, the Muskrats had retreated to their fort in an abandoned school bus, snuggled in the middle of a junkyard filled with stacks of crushed vehicles, aging electronics, and other unwanted things in the Windy Lake garbage dump. Without insulation and a windshield, the rusting bus wasn't much more than a windbreak.

The journey into the Mighty Muskrats' "castle" started in an old Bombardier that hunkered in the field just outside the piles of junked cars. In the aging snow van was a collection of pillows, posters, and junkyard pickings that would make it an attractive fort for any young person.

However, it was just a foyer.

Inside the rear engine compartment of the Bombardier, the Muskrats had camouflaged a tunnel, a reclaimed culvert, that led to the rear emergency door of the old school bus.

Within their hideaway, the young sleuths had removed most of the seats, and replaced them with bits and pieces of discarded furniture from the junkyard outside. A wooden table supported Chickadee's recycled, yellowing computer.

Otter picked up a beat-up guitar from one of the bus seats, turned sideways, and pushed against the wall.

Samuel sifted through a row of books protected from the elements by an upside-down trunk lid on the hood of the bus.

Atim tried to warm up by pacing around a salvaged incline bench, stubbing his toe on some barbells from a mismatched weight set.

The fort's heater, plugged into an extension cord that had been snaked through the junkyard from a distant electrical pole, coughed and ticked as it tried to heat a space too big for its little fan.

Chickadee waved at her computer with disgust. "Listen to this thing!" The ancient machine was also having its own little fit as its insides began to hum, whir, and spin. "I thought the cold was supposed to be good for electronics."

Sitting on the bench and holding his foot, Atim moaned. "T-t-too m-m-much of a g-g-good th-thing, I guess."

"Sheesh, big guy. It's not that cold!" Otter laughed as he leaned over and slapped his cousin on the shoulder.

Atim pretended to pinch a love handle that wasn't there. "I-it's b-because I got n-n-no b-body fat."

Chickadee smiled, sweetly. "It's all head fat. And it's all between your ears."

The computer stopped its rattling and let out a steady hum. Chickadee turned her attention back to the screen. She plugged in the USB modem that gave her access to the Internet.

"Mr. Penner said there are websites where people can find out about pills." Her fingers danced across the keyboard. "Okay, here it is, the Pill Identifier. They were kind of yellow-and-white, and clear, hey?"

Atim sat down on the weight bench and hugged himself. "M-M-Mr. P-penner said it was like a capsule, not a chewable. I think the heater is finally working."

Samuel leaned over Chickadee, looking at the screen. "Anything?"

"Yeah, I uploaded the pictures and these popped up. Check them out." She pointed at a few of the photos that resembled the bits found in the meat.

Sam leaned in, his hand on his chin, brow wrinkled, as he considered. "It looked like the yellow bit had writing on it."

Still sitting, Atim called over to his brother. "What's going on? What do you see?"

Sam spoke slowly as he read the screen, "It looks like it could be dram-a-mine or something that contains it, I guess. Says here, an anti…hista…mine compound used to counter naus…e…a."

Otter played softly on the guitar as his cousins studied the screen for clues. He chuckled. "Don't we have an Auntie Histamine?"

Chickadee was too focused to hear the joke. "Look! It says Dramamine is in Gravol. You know, the stuff Mom gives me if I'm feeling carsick."

Atim guffawed. "That's weird. Why would anyone want to give Gravol to a dog?"

Otter tried to get a laugh again. "It was a fast-moving race. Maybe someone has a lead dog that gets dizzy when it runs fast."

His cousins groaned.

Sam continued to read from the screen. "It says, 'blurred vision, constipation, drowsiness, or a dry mouth and throat may occur. If any of these effects persist or worsen, tell your doctor or pharmacist promptly.'"

Otter thought back to his experience with dog teams. "It always slows you down and can mess up the team when a dog needs to poop. Maybe someone was trying to cheat by plugging up their dogs?"

"Ever gross!" Chickadee pretended to hold her nose.

Otter laughed at his cousin's discomfort. "At the start of some races, where people use up to ten or more dogs, there is always a spot where the dogs all seem to want to go at once. You can have a whole stretch of nothing but dog poop. And then you have to scrape it off your skis if it gets frozen."

Chickadee gave him a look of disgust. "*Puh-lease* stop talking, Otter!"

Otter giggled.

"Muskwa couldn't run after he ate some of this. He was out," Sam said. "We don't really know how much he ate. But even a drowsy dog can't run."

Chickadee opened another tab in the browser and typed 'Dramamine Dogs.' "Well, it says people also give Gravol to dogs for car sickness. But check this out." She pointed at the screen. Atim and Sam leaned over.

"Wow!" Samuel was suddenly excited. Chickadee was pointing to a headline the search engine had produced: "Undercover Reporter Finds Greyhounds Drugged to Ensure Safe Bets."

Chickadee clicked on the link. The two Muskrats perused the story. Chickadee pointed at the accompanying photo. "Look at how skinny they are!"

Sam shrugged. "They're greyhounds. They all look like that. But it says here a trainer was giving Dramamine to his own dogs so they would run bad, and the odds would be raised against them. Then he would stop giving the dogs the drug, so they would run well and win the race."

Atim was confused. "What would that do? Why would he do that to his own dogs?"

Samuel was still reading the story when he answered. "Well, if the odds were against a dog winning, betting on it would get you a lot more money if it won."

"I still don't get it...." Atim's face twisted in consternation.

Sam thought quietly for a few seconds before turning to his brother. "Okay, you know that in every race there is a favorite, right?"

Atim nodded. "That's the racer most likely to win."

"Right. And you know that a long shot is a racer that people don't think is going to win? The odds are against it."

"Mmm-hmm."

Sam nodded. "So, if a long shot wins, it makes more money for the person who bet on it, right?"

Atim shrugged a shoulder in agreement.

Sam smiled at his brother. "So, the dog racer had a few dogs that were real fast, but before their first races, he gave them a slow-down pill—Dramamine."

Atim slapped his forehead in shock and surprise. "So, people thought they were long shots!"

Sam's head bobbed. "Yes! When people thought a dog was slow, the odds went up because it was a long shot. Then the dog's owner would *not* give the dog the slow-down pill, and the animal would show how fast it could really go."

Atim laughed. "Winning the race!"

Otter slapped his cousin's arm. "Yeah. But it's cheating."

Chickadee whistled. "A rigged race!"

Otter did a slow, low tone slide on the guitar. "But that's probably not what happened here, right? If you're going to drug your own dogs, why do it on the trail?"

The other Muskrats pondered Otter's point. Then they all nodded in agreement.

"Good point, Otter." Sam turned away from the computer screen. "But this news story pretty much nails it for me. I think, someone was messing with the youth race. And it could have been just an experiment to make sure the drugged meatballs work for the adult race."

Otter stopped tickling the strings and rapped his knuckles against the body of the guitar, making a dramatic thump. "We have to take this to Grandpa. He'll know what to do."

Chickadee looked over her shoulder at her cousin. "If someone is trying to fix the race, that's illegal, so we have to tell Uncle Levi too. He can tell the other band constables to keep an eye out."

"Good idea," Sam chimed in. "There are a lot of people in Windy Lake this week because of the race. And there are a lot of different entries who all want to win...."

Otter shook his head. He knew a lot of the mushers, or their children. "But that doesn't mean they will cheat!"

Chickadee shrugged sadly. "But it looks like someone is willing to. Says here, betting on dog racing in the South is a multimillion-dollar industry. Imagine someone making a million dollars on our little race in Windy Lake!"

Atim shook his head. "That's enough money to make people do some pretty bad things. Not just drug dogs."

Otter tapped on the guitar once again. "We really need to find out who is doing this, so we don't just go around accusing people."

All the Muskrats agreed.

Samuel stood and started putting on his toque and gloves. "Let's get back out there. The next step will be a tough one. We know what is happening. The hard part will be finding out who and turning up enough evidence to prove it!"

CHAPTER 5
Army Attack

"Hey, you kids, what are you doing?"

Startled, the Muskrats looked up to see their Uncle Jacob filling his truck with fuel. Due to the chilly air, the young sleuths had decided to stop off and warm up at one of the town's two gas stations. This one was affectionately known as the Station, or sometimes, the Drama Station.

Although he was often a little gruff, the young sleuths were happy to see their uncle. He always had a smile waiting in the background. As usual, he was dressed in rugged work clothes that looked and smelled as though they had spent a lot of time out on the land.

The snow under her feet crunched as Chickadee ran up and gave Uncle Jacob a hug. "Hi Uncle! Got anything today?"

The boy Muskrats had a different relationship with their Elder, who was often asked to act as a disciplinarian, or teacher, when it came to the young men in the family. For them, it was best to show more respect than familiarity with their traditional-thinking mentor.

Out of the boys, Otter knew him the best, having spent a few seasons working for the old man and his son, their cousin Jody. "Good to see you, Uncle. Where's Jody?"

"Ahh, he's been useless to me since he broke his leg. He's at the community hall, helping your auntie at the Traders Market. The family rented a table there."

Atim and Sam had never seen their Uncle Jacob when they lived in the city. They had a fairly fresh relationship with him that started when their parents moved back to the Windy Lake First Nation a few years before.

Sam waved at his uncle. "Jody still mad at us?"

Uncle Jacob was quiet for a few seconds. "He's happier now that Muskwa is back."

Chickadee smiled. "That's good."

Their uncle grunted in the way that their male Elders did when they didn't quite approve of what was going on. "Why did you drop off Muskwa and just leave without saying anything?"

The Muskrats all shrugged and rolled their eyes to the sky.

Their uncle grunted again. "You're all family.... You got to work it out." Sam opened his mouth to say something, but Uncle Jacob spoke first. "That's it.... You have to talk."

Sam nodded in agreement. "We'll talk to Jody, Uncle."

Uncle Jacob's hand cut through the air, closing the topic.

The gas pump thumped as it pulled in fuel.

Atim went to lean on the box of his uncle's truck but stopped when he realized how dirty it was. The sticky highway snow and the white limestone of Windy Lake had turned most of the red truck into a beige pink.

The tallest Muskrat checked out its load. His uncle's snowshoes and sled lay at the bottom, and a backpack and trapping supplies were piled in a corner by the cab. Through the truck's back window, a beat-up gun rack cradled a well-used, bolt-action rifle.

With one weather-worn hand still on the gas nozzle, Uncle Jacob reached into the back of his truck. He pulled up a selection of furred animals, each tied to a stained strand of blue nylon rope. "Nice day on the trapline. Few minks, a fisher, two muskrats. I'm going to give the muskrats to Pops once I've skinned them. So, if you want muskrat stew later, he'll have some."

The Mighty Muskrats grimaced. While muskrats cooked over a fire on a stick were not bad, muskrat stew always turned into a gray goo, often containing the boiled, grayed skeletons of the former rodents.

Atim flicked the hair out of his eyes and waved off the offer. "We're good. Thanks anyway."

Sam raised his eyebrows and whispered, "Did I just

hear my brother turn down food?"

Otter snickered.

The bell above the Station's restaurant door tinkled as it opened. The Muskrats and their uncle turned to look.

A squad of the Animal Army poured outside.

Although they emerged laughing, their faces turned harsh and disapproving once they noticed Uncle Jacob holding up his day's catch.

Chickadee thought it was obvious they were not locals. The activists were too well dressed. She lowered her eyes and murmured, "This could be trouble, Uncle."

Uncle Jacob's eyes widened. He looked at the other Muskrats. "Really?"

The boys nodded.

The older man chuckled. "Been a while since I was in a fight." He turned to observe the activists.

A number wore hoodies or jackets with the letters from city colleges or universities. A few of them were wearing matching snowsuits. They all seemed angry.

A young man, obviously a leader of the group, stepped forward, his straight, dark hair gelled into a rooster's comb. "Hey! Look at this." He pointed out the trapped animals to his friends, then sneered at Uncle Jacob. "You kill those yourself?"

Uncle Jacob raised the carcasses again. "Was a good day on the trapline. Nothing suffered, and the furs are in good condition."

"You feel proud of yourself?" the young man spewed back, stepping within a disrespectful distance from Uncle Jacob.

Uncle Jacob lifted an eyebrow, smiled, and lowered the animals back into the truck. He turned to face the young man. "Not any more than usual."

One of the other soldiers in the Animal Army got a little nervous. "Careful, Chet."

Chet sneered dismissively at the warning. "We said we came here for real action."

He nodded his chin aggressively at Sam. "Your old man is quite the savage."

Atim stepped protectively toward his younger brother. His eyes narrowed as he spoke, "We all are."

The gas pump clicked off as the truck's tank was finally filled. Uncle Jacob replaced the nozzle and screwed the gas cap back on. He had been amused with the altercation up to this point, but he was suddenly serious once the protestor spoke to the Muskrats. "You kids get in my truck. I'll go pay, but then I'll take you to Pop's after."

The tone in his voice mobilized the young sleuths. They jumped to comply. The touch of warning in Uncle Jacob's rumble also caused the activists to back out of his way. The four Muskrats hopped into the truck's cab and shut the door.

Their Elder made his way into the Station. Once his

back was turned, Chet, the leader of the young adults, spoke up. "Animals are not ours to experiment on, eat, wear, use, or abuse!"

The Muskrats watched as their uncle glanced over his shoulder and stepped through the gas station door.

Chickadee looked around at the angry people surrounding the truck. "Are they going to go away now?"

Otter shook his head. "Doesn't look like it."

The leader of the group and his buddy were whispering to each other, eyeing the corner of the truck box that held their uncle's furs.

Atim watched them angrily. "They better not try to do what I think they're going to do."

The young men glared when they noticed all the Muskrats turning to look at them through the gun rack. The activists stepped back, but began to yell, "Fur is murder! Fur is mur-der!"

Their friends followed suit, adding a tomahawk chopping motion. They all began to repeat the chant, with the rhythm people who have never been to a powwow use to mimic the Big Drum.

Chickadee covered her ears. "This is crazy! Why are they doing this?"

"Fur is mur-der! Fur is mur-der!"

Atim moved to open the door, but his brother stopped him. "Uncle's coming back."

"Fur is mur-der! Fur is mur-der!"

The other sleuths looked back through the truck's rear window to see their uncle sauntering across the parking lot. They rarely ever saw their uncle smirk, but it was obvious he found the activists humorous.

Chet, still in control of the group, stuck out an accusing finger at Uncle Jacob—from well outside of the bigger man's reach. "Your culture is murder!"

The other activists continued to shout, "Fur is murder! Fur is mur-der!"

Uncle Jacob stopped. "Most animals around here are killed by city people."

The young man snorted. "Civilized people don't hunt."

The Muskrats' uncle took a long look at Chet. They knew their Elder was deciding if the young man was worth his time. After appraising him, Uncle Jacob looked at the rest of the group. His voice rose so they could hear. "You all look like you're pretty used to electricity."

"What does that have to do with anything?" the young leader challenged.

The activists' chant stumbled to a stop.

Uncle Jacob pulled his keys out of his pocket, but with his other hand he swept a wide circle, indicating the breadth of lands around Windy Lake. "What is normal up here is bush, bush, and more bush. And a moose can outrun wolves in the trees. But you…," Uncle Jacob paused for effect, looking around the group, "…city people create fields where they don't belong, thousands of miles long, for hydro lines. A moose can't outrun the pack in a field. The electricity that keeps your house warm, helps wolves kill moose. Do you think they do it gently?"

"That's not our fault!!" The young activist raised his pointy finger at Uncle Jacob again.

"You sure?" Uncle Jacob said over his shoulder, as he opened the truck door.

Peeking inside, he saw four nervous cousins looking back. He gave them a small smile and shook his head a little, sharing his opinion of the protestors with his nieces and nephews. "You're going to have to squish over." He stepped into the truck, squeezing the four Muskrats into two seats, and closed the door.

The activists took up their chant again. "Fur is mur-der! Fur is mur-der!"

Uncle Jacob turned on the ignition and slowly moved forward. Two of the activists would not get out of the way. Another young man approached the driver's side door and spit on the window.

Uncle Jacob slammed on the breaks. He crooked his finger at the spitter, motioning him closer, rolling his window down an inch at the same time.

The protestor thought he'd have a better target and stepped forward with his lips pursed.

Uncle Jacob slammed his big shoulder into the door. It swung open and smacked the spitter flat on the forehead. He staggered back, almost tripping over the concrete base of the gas pumps. A few friends ran to stop him from falling.

The Muskrats' uncle rolled his window all the way down and leaned his head out. An activist still stood in front of the truck.

Uncle Jacob revved his engine. "You think I'm messing around, city boy? Get out of my way."

Wisely, the young man moved. Uncle Jacob rolled up his window, but as they drove away, a few more protestors lobbed gobs of phlegm.

Uncle Jacob looked over at his niece and nephews with a grin. "If I stayed ten minutes longer, they might have cleaned my truck."

CHAPTER 6

Muskrats and Marshmallows

"If there are any people who want to mess up the dog-sled race, I'd bet it's the Animal Army." Atim rolled bits of wood back into the flames with his firestick as the Mighty Muskrats, their grandfather, and Uncle Jacob discussed recent events.

When they arrived, Grandpa had been sitting at the campfire, alone, in his snowmobile suit of many colors. The snowsuit had been a Hudson's Bay favorite back in the 1970s. Since then, decade after decade, the Muskrats' Elder had managed to breathe new life into this winter fashion statement with corduroy, denim, and leather patches. They were now mixed with a few strips of duct tape.

Grandpa was relaxed in the cold, legs stretched out. His long, silver hair spilled over his shoulders as he leaned back in a rough wood Adirondack chair placed not too close to the flames.

Aware of the rules surrounding the winter fire, the Muskrats knew their Elder wouldn't give any advice on anything, unless he and Uncle Jacob had full cups of tea, and the Muskrats had their own hot beverage. A flurry of activity had occurred when they first arrived. Now, they all nestled around the little campfire in front of Grandpa's house. The two men relaxed with their tea, gazing down the hill at snow devils dancing across Windy Lake. The Muskrats blew marshmallows across cups of instant hot chocolate.

Uncle Jacob snorted. "Those crazy activists better be careful. There are more than a few young men who would've put them in their place, if they'd been at the Station. Bothering an old man like me." He smiled a little mischievously.

Atim hit himself in the forehead, mimicking the truck door hitting the protestor.

Everyone who had been there laughed into their cups.

Grandpa's eyes narrowed.

The snap and crackle of a vehicle coming down the road caused everyone to turn and look. Uncle Levi pulled into Grandpa's parking pad in his Windy Lake First Nation police truck. His door opened quickly, and he slid his big frame out, hitching up his belt once he landed. Levi was a slightly younger version of Uncle Jacob—wide shoulders, weather-worn hands, and a stoic demeanor. However, Uncle Levi's salt-and-pepper hair was a sharp, military cut, and his Windy Lake band constable uniform was always crisp and clean.

He gave a quick wave to everyone as he walked up, but then he looked at his brother. "So, causing trouble again?"

Uncle Jacob's eyebrows rose, and he allowed a slight smirk to flitter across his face, before his expression instantly switched to an almost-sincere look of consternation. "I have no idea what you're talking about, Levi! Did something happen?"

The Muskrats giggled, stopping quickly when Uncle Levi glanced at them.

Uncle Levi took off his Windy Lake Police baseball cap, scratched his head, replaced it, and spoke seriously. "Those Animal Army nuts came to the office and said you assaulted one of them with a truck door."

Uncle Jacob was smiling broadly now. "Oh, my goodness! Was there blood?"

"Well…no. But he'll have a pretty square bruise in the middle of his forehead for a while." Uncle Levi tightened his lips. "They wanted to press charges, but the guy with the bruise dropped it when I told them they'd have to come back in a few months and testify."

Uncle Jacob shrugged. "Hmm. It was just unfortunate timing. He was leaning forward to spit into my truck, just as I happened to be opening the door."

Atim's voice held a touch of anger as he spoke through a chocolate mustache, "They had us surrounded, Uncle Levi. Chickadee was scared."

Chickadee picked up some snow and tossed it at her cousin. "You were freaked out too, tough guy."

Atim held up his hands to block the tossed snow. "Okay. Okay. I was freaked out too."

Otter's brow was furrowed. "I didn't get why they were so angry."

The thought hung in the air as they waited for the oldest among them to weigh in.

The air was crisp but felt packed full of oxygen. The fire crackled in the gray of a winter afternoon in the North.

Grandpa went from leaning back in the wooden chair, to sitting forward, elbows on knees, rubbing his hands before the fire. "As I have taught you before, a land, and the activities of collecting that land's food, water, and other resources creates a way of life. When a group of people live that way of life, after a few generations, that lifestyle becomes their culture...."

Otter continued. "And when they reach for the stars, and the stars reach down, that becomes their ceremony."

Sam was eager to hear something new. "You are the land you live on, hey, Grandpa?"

"Creation's gifts and teachings are in our lands." He lip-pointed to the Muskrats' uncles. "I taught that way of seeing the world to these two and their brothers and sisters."

Grandpa rubbed his jaw as he spoke thoughtfully, "Anger is often a luxury. It is rarely a need."

The old man looked around at the Muskrats. "A city is like an anthill. It is a landscape made by people, for people. In the city, people live their lives with someone else getting their food from the farm—sometimes cooking it even—and then cleaning up after. Other people build their houses, make their clothes, and…take away their poop." Grandpa snickered.

Everyone chuckled.

Chickadee looked around the group and felt a warm glow. The other Muskrats were just as happy as she was to sit with their Elders.

After a lull, Grandpa filled the silence. "When their concerns for food and water and shelter and clothes are met, the city people begin to worry about other things, lesser needs. And when those *needs* are met by those around them…then they move on to their *wants*. And sometimes, after so many generations of living that way, their *wants* seem like *needs*. And so, they fight about their wants, as though they are needs."

Sam thought about what was said. "But how does that turn into anger at a dogsled race?"

Uncle Jacob threw up his arm with disgust. "They're crazy!! They won't stop until everyone is living their way."

Uncle Levi chided his brother. "They are off center,

but they think they are doing right."

Uncle Jacob scoffed. "Spitting on my truck?"

Grandpa held up his hand and leaned back in his chair. "You two are setting a poor example for your niece and nephews." The family's Elder gave a stern look to his sons.

The two men shifted in their seats, but they held their opinions in respectfully. They were in their father's yard, after all.

After a cleansing silence, Grandpa sat forward. He pointed at Sam and then the rest of the Muskrats in turn. "If you're curious, I want you to find out."

Sam sat up straight, his face concerned. "Find out why they're so angry?"

Grandpa nodded. "It's not my place to speak for them. And…if you care, it is your place to seek understanding." The old man deliberately met the eyes of each of his young grandchildren.

Chickadee tightened her lips, and she looked down as she spoke, "But they're older and bigger than us, Grandpa."

"Then you may need an ally. They are a group, but that does not mean that they all have the same feelings and thoughts about everything. Maybe there is one among them who is not so angry. Maybe someone who doesn't think spitting at a truck full of children is a good idea."

Otter was thoughtful as he spoke, "They're city people. They are so different from us."

Grandpa shook his head. "There are always places where we can agree to meet together. It seems to me these city people think more like us than we give them credit for…on some things."

Otter's face filled with confusion. "What do you see, Grandpa?"

"I see people who also view our animal cousins as family. They do not see our cousins as far beneath them, not separate. They see them as another shade of living. That is a connection."

Uncle Jacob let out a slightly surprised "Ho!" of agreement.

Everyone else nodded at the thought.

Atim flicked the hair out of his eyes as he leaned forward, staring into the fire. "They have a website, I bet. Chickadee could check out their web page to find out about them."

Grandpa shook his head. "Knowledge is good, but wisdom is better. Wisdom is good, but understanding is better. The web page is not a guest on our territory. The people are."

Uncle Jacob, suddenly, shifted his weight. "Pretty rude guests!"

Grandpa looked at his older son. His voice held a touch of reproach. "Then it is in the best interests of our people to seek better understanding of what they are capable of."

Uncle Jacob and Uncle Levi raised their eyes, appreciating their father's thought.

Sam pinched his chin. "I thought wisdom was the most valuable."

Grandpa nodded, but then shook his head. "Wisdom is valuable. But the ability to find understanding is a gift that all Creation enjoys. Have you ever seen the look of joy on a baby's face when they understand something new?"

With smiles, the Muskrats nodded.

Grandpa smiled back. "In some ways, you can think of wisdom as light. But it is understanding that carries the light. Understanding is what wisdom travels through. Once you understand these guests to our territory, you will have the knowledge of how to treat them appropriately. Hopefully, you will do that with wisdom, and through Creation's laws of Kindness and Respect."

Uncle Jacob smirked. "Even if the right decision is kicking them out?"

Grandpa nodded seriously. "Yes. Even if the right decision is asking them to leave."

The family sat in silence while Grandpa's last words hung in the air. As the fire snapped and glowed, chocolate mustaches grew, thermoses emptied, and a family pondered.

After a while, Sam started to fidget.

"Ants in your pants, or what?" Grandpa poked Sam,

knowing full well his grandson was a box of questions.

Sam looked at the sky, picking his first query. "What if they are the ones sabotaging the race?"

Grandpa raise an eyebrow back at him. "Would a better understanding of them help you figure that out?"

Sam snickered. "Yeah, I guess. Of course."

Grandpa spread his hands wide and pretended to push something back at his grandchildren. "Then it looks like you have work to do."

Uncle Levi shook his head a little, a worried expression crossing his brown face. "What's this about sabotaging a race?"

The head band constable was suddenly flooded with four excited summaries of the Muskrats' case about a possible attempt to rig the Windy Lake International Sled Dog Race.

Grandpa chuckled and slapped his leg. "You asked for it!"

Uncle Levi handled the deluge of incoming info with his usual calm demeanor. When the last of the Muskrats mumbled to a stop, their uncle lip-pointed at Otter. "Where is the hamburger now?"

Otter answered. "Most of it is in Grandpa's freezer. Some of it was sent to a lab by Mr. Penner."

Uncle Levi lip-pointed at Chickadee. "Why do you think it's sabotage?"

Chickadee sat up straight on her stump and spread

her mittened hands. "The little pieces of plastic are bits of pills. Mr. Penner helped us figure that out with the microscope. And we think the pills are Dramamine, which some news stories say has been used to mess with dog races down South."

Uncle Levi was impressed. He thrust his chin toward Atim. "Why do you think this Animal Army did this?"

Atim was quiet for a moment, his brother always had great ideas, and Atim figured he was due one. "They… have a passion…that could push them to do something like this."

Uncle Levi looked at the floor, thoughtfully. "It would seem they do. What about timing? Does it fit?"

The largest of the Muskrats pulled back his head, confused. "What do you mean?"

Otter poked at his cousin. "I think he means, were they in the correct place at the correct time to be able to toss the burger balls into the teen race." Otter shrugged. "We'll need to figure that out."

Uncle Levi nodded thoughtfully, then he lip-pointed at Sam. "Is the Animal Army your only lead?"

Sam shook his head. "They can't be. There are other people who care about the dogsled race. Mr. Penner said it was likely there would be people betting on the Windy Lake International, and wherever there was money, there would be shenanigans."

Uncle Jacob tapped his lips with his thick forefinger.

"We wouldn't want any shenanigans."

Sam shook his head seriously. "One single shenanigan could blow the whole race."

Otter's eyes got big. "Not just for this year. A shenanigan could affect the race for years to come."

Uncle Levi cocked his head at the seriousness of the thought. "If there is a shenanigan at the center of this...it could create a ripple effect. Then you'll have a lot more...."

Sam poked a finger skyward. "I believe the correct plural form of shenanigans is shenanigi."

Atim looked at the ground and said quietly, "*Shenanigans*. It's a funny word."

His cousins and Elders looked at him, then chuckled in agreement.

Uncle Levi cleared his throat, took off his band constable cap, scratched his head, and then put the hat back on. "If this is a real attempt to cheat in the adult race, I hope you Muskrats don't mind if we get involved."

Sam laughed as he gave his uncle's arm a nudge. "All good, Uncle. We could use any help we can get!"

Uncle Levi smiled a little smile that soon disappeared. "If this does involve money, the level of bad guy involved could be higher than what we are used to around here." He looked around the group. "I've told you Muskrats to be careful before, but I really mean it this time. If there is big money involved, we could be dealing with organized crime—big-time gangsters from the South."

"You don't think it might be the Animal Army, Uncle?" Otter spoke as he tried to get the last few drops of hot chocolate into his mouth.

Uncle Levi watched the fire for a moment. "Well… they're still suspects, but there are a lot of new people in town. There's a lot of interest in the race. I'll tell the RCMP, and, once we all start digging around, who knows what might come out of the woodwork?"

Grandpa spoke in a low rumble as he filled his cup with tea from his thermos. The steam disappeared into the cloudy afternoon atmosphere. "Why don't you Muskrats start by learning to understand the people of the Animal Army? Maybe you can help your Uncle Levi by finding out more about them and possibly crossing them off the suspect list."

Atim smacked his hands together. "We'll figure out the Animal Army, Grandpa."

Sam spoke next. "I wonder if we know someone that they know, so we could maybe talk to one of them."

Chickadee piped up. "A lot of them seem to be university and college students. Denice went to university in the city for a bit. Maybe we should talk to her!"

Sam pointed at Chickadee in approval of her idea. "Or Harold! Do you know where they are?"

Atim jumped up. "The flour-packing contest! The qualifying heat is tonight! That's where she'll be! We got to go. We can't miss the finals. Jeff is in them!"

Uncle Levi tightened his lips and wagged a finger. "Be careful! This Animal Army may not be the mafia, but they do seem angry. Don't face off with them. Stick to gathering information and don't go anywhere where you'd be alone with them."

Grandpa nodded in agreement with his son.

Chickadee's eyes grew wide. "You don't have to tell us! The last time we met them, it was a nightmare!"

CHAPTER 7
Flour Power

"*Aahhh!* His legs are going to break!!!"

Otter had climbed on top of Atim in his excitement, hanging off his cousin like a backpack, pumping the air with his free fist.

Sam and Chickadee screamed, "Go! Go! Go!"

The flour packing contest was a feat of strength and one of the most attended events at the Fur Trappers Festival. Where the grueling gauntlet began, sixty-pound flour sacks, tied in pairs to provide balance, would be very carefully placed onto each contestant. After each round, volunteers added to the burden by gently placing more sixty-pound bags onto the bent backs of the challengers. The mass increased with each round, and the losers dropped under their load, or never lifted it past the starting line. The winners often carried the weight of a small car across the fifty-foot stretch of the race.

The sun had set but the event area was illuminated by several floodlights. A corralled crowd screamed from behind orange snow fences on either side of the raceway.

Jeff was one of the Muskrats' biggest cousins. Today, he wore his lucky blue jeans, his favorite AC/DC T-shirt, and a special moose hide jacket that their grandmother handmade for him long ago.

Jeff wobbled as he fought against inertia and gravity. The white flour sacks stood six layers thick on his shoulders, towering above his head, hanging off of him on either side, and seemingly ready to slide down his back. A canvas strap stretched out from the load and around Jeff's forehead. The entire gargantuan heap was resting on the top of his spine.

The Muskrats' favorite contestant was a giant, even in a family of big men. His wide, thick shoulders made a stable foundation for the great load of flour bags. With a tiny shuffle of his left foot, Jeff and his baggage moved—another halting shamble, then a toe-scuff forward, followed by a sliding step.

Each year's contest proved it was the legs that betrayed. Jeff's mighty columns were spread wide, pushing the weight into the earth, but shaking uncontrollably. He shuffled forward an inch, another shuffle, another inch. He tried to lift a whole foot, but his other leg moaned under the pressure. He put his foot down quickly, gaining little ground, but not enough to make it worth the effort. Jeff slid a foot forward, then a scuff, another skate step.

Sam imagined that the spray paint on the ground marking the end of the competition would seem like a wall to his giant cousin. "How does he do it?!"

Chickadee covered her eyes for a second with her beaded leather mitt. She couldn't help but think of the year a contestant's load was put on lopsided. The guy's fall to one side resulted in a broken leg. A shiver went down her spine, and she tried to shake away the memory of the fractured bone poking out of muscle. "Lookin' good, cousin! You can do it!" she screamed.

Atim ignored Otter on his back, even as his little cousin smacked his scalp in excitement. The biggest of the Muskrats watched Jeff's technique. His giant cousin's eyes were laser-focused on the finish line. Jeff had come in second last year, and Atim knew what it meant to want the gold so bad, you could taste it. "You got this Jeff-y! Just do it! Do it! Do it! Do it!"

Otter was so excited he could almost pee, but he didn't think Atim would like that.

The whole family was sure this was Jeff's year. Before the race, the Muskrats' big cousin had seemed confident. Jeff had rolled his shoulders, given Otter a head rub for good luck, pointed at the end of the race, and said, "That flour is already over there, cuz."

It was a pretty cool moment.

Now, Otter slapped Atim's head to send Jeff energy. "You're awesome, Jeff. We love you! You're already there!"

Jeff's toes seemed to claw him forward, little by little. His face had turned a bright red.

Otter caught a whiff of smoke. The kind that comes from one of those big, chewed cigars he'd seen in old movies. Tortured tobacco. He looked across the crowd from his perch atop Mount Atim.

The carrot-sized stogie was stuck in a greedy smile. It smoldered under a freshly purchased, fox pelt hat, which gave an already gigantic head the appearance of a small, furry moon. The hat was out of place on the muscular man. His long, black coat and the suit underneath obviously came from a fancy shop in the city. He held a wad of cash in his hand. As Jeff took each tortured step, young men from the mine would come up, whisper in the man's ear, and give him more money. He was obviously very happy about it. Eventually, the dandy lifted the currency and waved it, looking, not at Jeff, but at someone in the fenced-in crowd on the opposite side of the track.

Otter couldn't figure out who the money was being flexed at, until he saw a local ruffian flash an obscene gesture at the city slicker.

Eddie never graduated from Windy Lake High School, mostly because he was from a rough family in town that did not value education. He wore a puffy, shiny jacket. His long, black hair was pulled back into a single ponytail, and the "suit" underneath his outerwear was denim. Everyone knew that when Eddie was in trouble on the reserve, he would disappear into the city for a while. Apparently, he was back. Otter noticed Eddie also had a fistful of cash, and that young men—most from around town, but some from the mine—came by, whispered in his ear, and handed him more.

Otter reached down and plucked the toque off a cheering Samuel's head. Thinking the toque was falling off, Sam slapped his own skull quickly. Otter stifled a chuckle. His cousin looked at the ground, but seeing nothing there, he glanced up at Otter holding the hat.

Sam snatched it back. "What did you do that for? Jeff's halfway there!"

Otter lip-pointed at Eddie and shouted over the noisy crowd, "Check that out."

Sam looked in that direction, then yelled back, "What?! Eddie?"

Otter nodded and lip-pointed again, just as another man came up and stuffed some money in the local bully's hand. "Look fishy?"

Sam nodded, putting on his toque. "So fishy, it stinks. But there's nothing we can do now. Wait until later."

Otter's lips tightened, but he pulled his eyes away from Eddie's transactions.

Jeff was almost at the end. He had leaned forward, not much, but just enough to force his feet to stumble toward the finish line. He achieved a kind of shuffle step, steadily moving him over the ground.

Gaining momentum, the load seemed to want to pass him. Jeff stopped and pushed back against the mountain of powdered wheat.

The Muskrats held their breath.

Jeff wobbled, but when the wobble leaned him forward, their big cousin started shuffling again. Picking up steam, he was soon across the finish line, earning a place in the finals of the Windy Lake Flour Packing Race.

The Muskrats were ecstatic.

Otter slid down Atim and then gave him a big bear hug, lifting him off his feet.

Sam and Chickadee grasped forearms and jumped up and down, up and down. "He did it! He did it!"

The happy detectives continued to celebrate as they left the raceway with the rest of the crowd. The finals would happen the next night.

Samuel was walking in front of Otter but turned when his cousin tapped him on the back. "Should we tell Uncle Levi what we saw, Sam?"

Chickadee and Atim stopped talking and looked back. "What did you see?" asked Chickadee.

Sam explained what they had seen Eddie doing. "I'm guessing, he was taking bets."

Otter shook his head. "And he wasn't the only one." He went on to explain the apparent rivalry between the well-dressed man and Eddie. "I wouldn't say they were friends."

"Two rival bad guys taking bets on the flour packing semi-finals?! This sounds like something we should tell Uncle Levi." Atim's eyebrows showed his concern.

The rest of the Muskrats agreed.

Chickadee turned to Otter. "What did Mr. Fancy Pants look like?"

Otter squinted at her. "Like he was rich. He was from the city for sure. Kind of looked like a guy from those old gangster movies."

"Hey! You Muskrats! What are you doing?!" The young sleuths froze for a moment. Then they turned around slowly to see where the gruff voice had come from. But after seeing who was yelling at them, they laughed and ran to meet two of their favorite older cousins.

Denice and Harold were both a few years out of high school. Being cousins of the same age group, they had herded together, much like the Muskrats did now. It made for a very close bond between them and the other cousins that entered the family at the same time.

Chickadee ran up and gave Harold, who was usually at university in the city, a big hug. "Harold, what are you doing here?"

Harold had always been flamboyant and living in the city gave him a freedom that small-town life in Windy Lake sometimes curtailed. A strip of purples and greens edged the trim of his hair. He wore a parka that looked like it was purchased at the local Co-op, but underneath were duds fresh from the city mall. "I did a lot of beading and sewing this fall. I chipped in for a craft table with the aunties. Denice and I are on our way to help the aunties set it up, so it looks nice when the hall opens in the morning. I hope to make some money for Christmas."

Sam smiled. "What are you up to, Denice?"

Denice was a rising youth leader in Windy Lake. She had a strong spirit and was known to be a little rough and tough. But she was also a beautiful Cree woman, with long black hair, dark eyes, high cheekbones, and a bright smile. "I'll help set up too, but I figured I better stop first and pick this guy up. He's been in the city so long, might not know where he's going."

"Did you see Jeff place in the finals?" Atim skipped in circles around the group, still excited from the competition.

Harold shook his head. "Missed it. Was it good?"

Atim fell to his knees and threw two handfuls of snow in the air. "It was *awesome!*"

As they all walked over the crunchy snow toward the community hall, each Muskrat gleefully chimed in with their play-by-play of the flour packing contest. Then they all agreed to meet at the craft table in the community hall when it opened in the morning.

CHAPTER 8

Trading Traps

The morning dawned, revealing a sparkling winter's day. As promised, the Mighty Muskrats headed to the trade and craft show early. Harold met them at the entrance, eager to see their reactions to his handiwork.

"Our table's in the corner with the other traditional crafters." Harold pointed toward the back of the room. Once inside the community hall, they all had to wait for a moment as their eyes adjusted from the bright glittering snow to the dimmer, overhead lights.

The large, rectangular hall was filled with rows of tables, each with products or samples or pamphlets, as well as a team of hawkers to sell them. Everything from firetrucks for communities to mukluks for babies was sold at the Windy Lake Trade Show. The room was already filled with a low murmur, as vendors began to haggle with arriving customers.

Following their older cousin, Atim, Chickadee, Otter, and Sam did their best to fill their pockets with free candy from the trade booths using sweets as bait.

The Muskrats' late grandmother had been known for her beading and leatherwork. She had often won the top prizes at the Trappers Festival. Her spirit still inspired her children and grandchildren to take up and excel at the traditional craft.

People from all over the North came to sell their crafts, so there were Dene, Anishinaabe, Oji-Cree, and, of course, Cree patterns.

Along the way, Chickadee pointed out some beadwork. "See that flower? That's the Chartier family flower. Isn't it beautiful?"

The boys nodded.

"It's pretty, but what's with all the flowers?" Atim asked.

Chickadee picked up another moccasin with dark blue and light blue flowers, their petals connected circles beaded onto its toe. She held it out to show to him. "Back in the old days, it was the women who made the clothes, and they beaded what they loved—flowers. So, the flowers became almost like family flags."

"Hey, you two! Over here! Hurry up!" Otter and the others had arrived at the family's booth.

Atim and Chickadee replaced the leather shoe and jogged over.

When they got to the family table, Atim picked up a toddler's slipper with beadwork on the upper. He leaned over and whispered to Chickadee, "So, is this our flower?"

The slipper was made of softened deer hide, with a black rabbit fur cuff at the ankle. Beaded onto the toe of the slipper was a flower, with four large, turquoise petals married together by a round, soft orange center. Dark and light green leaves and vines curled around and framed the flower.

Chickadee took the slipper and ran her fingertips over the little glass orbs with affection. "This was Grandma's flower. Our moms and the aunties could tell you how many beads of each color it takes to make one. When people see this flower, they always know someone from our family made it."

Harold leaned in between them. "That's why, if you ever buy a beaded jacket from an old Cree woman, you should ask her for a list of families she's feuding with." He snickered.

Atim's and Chickadee's eyes grew big before they laughed out loud.

With a flick of his head, Harold indicated they should follow him. He led them to the other end of the aunties' craft table. "I wanted to show you these, Chickadee."

With a flourish, Harold pointed out a set of beaded jewelry, hair clips, bow ties, necklaces, and other fashion items that many would certainly not consider traditional, but they had been decorated using traditional beadwork, feather, and bone.

Chickadee gasped as she saw them. "Oh, my gosh! Harold, this is artwork."

Her older cousin gave her a quick hug, obviously pleased with her response.

Chickadee looked over her shoulder at the other Muskrats, milling about and blocking walking traffic. "Boys! Check these out."

Otter whistled. "Niiice work, cousin."

Sam held up an interesting piece. It was made out of coiled silver wire, with beads placed in just the right way to create a traditional pattern. It wasn't heavy, but it was large enough to remind Sam of an Egyptian collar. "This is amazing. It's like the stuff they call *haute couture*."

Atim lifted an eyebrow at his brother. "Hot what?"

Sam just chuckled and shook his head.

Harold waved off the compliment and then lightly touched his cousin's shoulder. "*Haute couture*, Atim, kind of means high fashion. But I can't take all the credit. My university friend, Tripp, he's Anishinaabe and an amazing artist. My stuff just echoes his, but he does it so much better."

The auntie behind the table, looking like a middle-aged Chickadee, watched the young sleuths examining their older cousin's artwork.

Denice lip-pointed at a ribbon pinned to the curtain

that separated the booths. "You guys should be proud of your cousin. He's won in the Fusion category."

Atim whooped. The other Muskrats patted Harold on the back and offered their congratulations.

Harold gave a little curtsy and then held his hand out to their Elder. "I couldn't have done it without the aunties."

Their auntie nodded at Harold with appreciation. She gestured to the Muskrats. "You kids could learn something from your cousin about how to take the city people's stuff and make it Cree."

Harold blushed at the compliment.

Suddenly, Denice whispered, "His stuff is better than *those*!"

The whole family looked at her. By glancing out of the edge of her eyes, she indicated a woman walking by.

"Don't look!" Denice hissed when everyone turned.

Trying to be discreet, but not accomplishing it, the Muskrats snatched a quick glance at what was on the woman's feet. It was a pair of MetroMuks factory-made boots with rubber soles and mukluk-like tops.

Chickadee looked confused. "Lots of people have those."

Denice scoffed, "Yeah, that's the problem."

Their auntie sighed. "That company formed when you kids were just toddlers and Grandma was still alive. When you were small, Mom would take what she couldn't sell at the Trappers Festival down to the city to make Christmas money. She was a hard worker, our mother. She sold to the middle-class people in the downtown mall."

"Until they came along!" Denice threw her hands skyward.

Their aunt continued. "When MetroMuks started up, a lot of people celebrated. It was owned by an Indigenous man, and many of the people who worked for him were Indigenous. And he used Indigenous designs in the beadwork...."

Denice thrust one of their moccasins in front of the Muskrats and pointed to it. "That's beadwork, not that factory stuff!"

Their auntie continued, unperturbed. "Everyone thought he was doing a good thing. But your grandmother noticed the difference right away. People weren't coming to the kiosk she rented with the other ladies to buy their genuine traditional stuff. MetroMuks had a whole store, and all the Canadians were flocking to it."

"Pfffhhhttt!" Denice rolled her eyes.

"Eventually, there just weren't enough people buying the traditional footwear to pay for the kiosk." Their auntie shrugged sadly.

Otter shook his head. "But there's a lot of difference, isn't there? Your beadwork is so much better and some of the hide you use is home tanned, so it has that cool smell."

Their auntie nodded but then lifted a shoulder.

"They have rubber soles, and you don't have to put those MetroMuks outside to cool and keep them dry. And that smell is comforting to you because it reminds you of home and your grandmother. City people don't feel the same way."

Chickadee was watching the woman as she walked away. "Really, the MetroMuks are made of leather, they look First Nation, and they do have some beading. So, from a fashion perspective...."

Atim raised a fist to the air. "But they aren't the same thing! Shouldn't we be mad at the guy who invented them? He took away Grandma's business!"

Their auntie tightened her lips and gave Atim the look that said she wanted her nephew to be more kind. "Everything is always in motion. Everything changes. Did he do wrong by making a product that fits city people better? Did he do wrong by making a better life for himself, his family, and his workers? Isn't that what we're all supposed to do?"

Samuel gazed skyward, thoughtfully. "I imagine the same thing happened with canoes. First Nation craftsmen understood the materials around them, when they were ready to collect, and how to create the birch bark canoe. It was how everyone and their stuff got around for thousands of years. But now, hardly anyone knows how to make birch bark canoes."

Their auntie's hands worked as she spoke, sorting the

moccasins, mitts, slippers, and mukluks that their family had for sale. "I think the MetroMuk owners realized they were changing things, so they tried to help traditional leatherworkers. They even developed classes to teach younger people how to do leatherwork."

"Did it work?" Chickadee asked as she helped sort the products.

Their Elder's lips tightened, then she waggled her head. "Yes and no. Before the company started, every family had leatherworkers. But when people stopped buying, it wasn't worth the effort for young people to learn the craft. Once factory-made moccasins and mukluks were available, there was no way to restart family leatherworking, like winter in the old days did."

Atim clenched his fists in front of his face. "It still makes me mad. He shouldn't have done it."

The Muskrats' aunt gave Atim a stern look. "Everything changes as time flows. Some of it good, some of it bad. Most of it falls somewhere in the middle. Everyone is just trying to stay above that flow." She regarded her nieces and nephews. With a sweep of her arm, she took in the rest of the world. "Sometimes, people start down a river without understanding where it leads. When you look at another person's actions, even if they produce results you do not like, you must look at the heart of the person and ask yourself, 'Why did they do that? Did they have bad intentions in their heart? Or were they just trying to stay above the flow of time's river?'"

Denice shook her head, angrily, but said nothing.

Noticing the gesture, the old auntie spoke directly to her. "The MetroMuks may have been the final blow to the old way of trading leatherwork, but it was those"— she pointed at Denice's sneakers—"that really started the changes. Why aren't you wearing moccasins if this makes you so mad?"

Denice's anger ebbed. Slightly chagrined, she shrugged.

Their auntie nodded. She went back to sorting products on the family's trade table, but then lip-pointed toward the door. "Now, get out of here. You're scaring away the few customers there are. No. Wait. Go to the Co-op and get me some chocolate."

The Muskrats' auntie went to get her purse.

CHAPTER 9

Co-op Ejection

The Muskrats hit the Co-op's outer door at a jog. Its thin, steel frame swung open with a smack as it hit the layers of cardboard that had been duct taped there to protect the back wall from damage caused by people who entered in a hurry. The doorknob had been removed, or never was installed. Instead, there was a yellow nylon string for pulling the door open, or closed. A blue-black rag was stuffed in the hole to prevent a cold draft.

Atim opened the inner door with a flourish and motioned for his fellow sleuths to step inside.

Once in the warm air, the Muskrats were in a makeshift hallway. It was formed by a long row of dusty cases of plastic pop bottles, which partially prevented the winter wind from blowing into the larger store interior. Rounding this partition, they allowed the sights and smells of the Windy Lake Co-op to wash over them.

They smiled their hellos to the cashier, and she pointed with her lips to the back of the store. "City people," she announced, then blinked.

The Muskrats glanced at each other as they processed the new info.

Windy Lake was on the highway, but it was still remote enough to be subject to higher prices and cost fluctuation due to supply and change in the variety of goods. This made it standard practice for the Muskrats to peruse the entire store on every visit, checking for items that had disappeared, or prices that might have fallen as supply to the community increased. They paraded, single file, down the first aisle, scanning the shelves.

As they approached the toothpaste and cold remedy area, they heard loud voices debating angrily.

Sam turned and raised his eyes at the others. He mouthed, "City people?"

Atim nodded.

The Muskrats moved closer to the shelf where the voices were coming from. They stopped to listen.

"If we want to make allies, we can't act like that!" The young woman's voice was passionate and certain.

"Millie, they torture animals for their skins. They run dogs until they're dead! Why do we need them as allies?"

"First, those are both exaggerations. And second, there's a bigger picture in all this!"

"I told you before we left, I came here to end this, not

talk. If we destroy their audience, we'll bring the whole thing down."

"Now you make me wonder what you were doing for the two days before we showed up."

Millie's comment was met with silence. Her tone was gentler but adamant when she spoke again. "You can't act like a bully. You'll lose half the group. The girls are with me on this!"

Again, silence.

Millie sighed. "Well…I got what I need."

The Muskrats heard a small squeak from her sneakers as she turned on the tile floor and walked away.

Otter closed his eyes as he waited and listened for some indication that the owner of the male voice had left.

Atim stood on his tiptoes and stretched his neck to see over the divider. When he came back down, he whispered, "He's just standing there, kind of hunched over."

Chickadee tapped on his elbow. "Keep looking."

Atim used Otter's head and Sam's shoulder to help raise himself higher. The two smaller boys struggled to stay standing. Otter's hat was squished down over his eyes. He waved his arms, trying to maintain his balance. Sam's shoulder wavered as he winced in pain. Chickadee shushed them even as she giggled.

Atim lowered himself releasing the smaller Muskrats. "He picked up something and left."

Sam raised his eyebrows, rubbed the feeling back into

his shoulder, and leaned over to see the end of the aisle. "Nobody."

The Muskrats all exhaled and walked to the end of the shelves.

"What did he grab?" Sam asked.

Atim tapped a box on the shelf. "This one, I think."

Otter grabbed the box as the others gathered around him to see.

Sam got excited as he read its label. "It contains Dramamine! The slow-down drug."

Atim took the package and flipped it back and forth. "This doesn't look like what Mom gives us."

Sam shrugged. "It's generic."

Chickadee laughed. "The cheaper version."

Otter glanced at the front of the store. "Put it back. They could be leaving."

Sam grabbed the box from Atim and put it on the shelf.

"Hey!" Atim looked disgruntled.

Chickadee slapped him on the shoulder. "Let's go! We have to see what they look like."

The Muskrats quickly made their way down the next aisle. In a moment, they were in sight of the cashier's station.

Chickadee hissed. "There they are!"

The young sleuths suddenly became interested in the products nearest to them.

Chickadee hissed again. "Use the corner of your eye!"

The Muskrats all slid their eyes sideways to the people going through the cashier lane.

One was Chet, the leader of the Animal Army, as they had all suspected. His coifed and glued hair hung over his forehead like a rooster's comb.

The young woman named Millie stood beside him. She pulled her dark hair back over her shoulder, making it easier to see her face.

The cashier made the inane chatter everyone in Windy Lake makes when they're speaking to someone from out of town. "Have you been to the snake pits? It's winter now, but you can still get a good view of the lake and the escarpment, the big cliff, in the distance."

The two activists nodded, and made similar, polite conversation, as they paid. The lady noticed the Muskrats as the pair left.

"That's that." Atim shrugged and stretched.

Sam blinked and threw up his arms. "We may now have a new main suspect!"

His older brother weighed the idea, then nodded in agreement.

Chickadee tugged on Samuel's winter coat. "You think he bought that stuff to put in more meatballs?"

Otter shook his head. "Don't know. Maybe he just has a bad tummy."

Sam lip-pointed at Otter. "Doctor Otter is right. We don't know, but I wonder…. Chet hates the dog race."

"He's got a lot of passion. He doesn't care about anyone around here. So, what does it matter to him?" Atim wondered aloud.

Otter smiled. "Oooorrr, he gets a funny stomach on long car rides."

The others chuckled.

Thoughtfully, they all turned and walked back to end of the aisle they had emerged from. They resumed their standard route through the store, perusing the shelves that were their most physical connection to the world outside Windy Lake.

They loved the smell of everything newly shipped in, from the chemical pinch of rubber boots to the throat-clogging dust of linens, to the oily sniff of tools and chain-saws. And then, there was the grocery side of the store with its long-cooled baked goods; its bruised, sweet-smelling fruit; the copper tang of frozen blood and meat; and then the acrid tang of chlorine and cleaning goop.

Toward the end of their route, the young sleuths came across a large man in a dirty, blue jumpsuit tossing assorted soda pop and bottled juices into a display fridge. He looked over his shoulder as they walked past. Upon recognizing her, he turned and doffed his hat. "Ms. Chickadee."

With a giggle, Chickadee stopped. "Hey, Pop Guy. How's the delivery route?"

The other Muskrats carried on, scanning the shelves. They were used to Chickadee being friendly with anyone who passed through Windy Lake. Her cheeky smile always caused others to smile back. She caught up with her cousins a couple of minutes later.

When they reached the end of the last aisle, they circled.

"Did you see anything?" Sam looked around the group.

Chickadee shook her head. "Did you see the price of chicken parts?"

Atim was suddenly curious.

Chickadee looked at him as she spoke. "My mom says the price of food is going up. She says meat here is a lot more expensive than in the city."

Sam pinched his chin, thoughtfully. "Everything is shipped in, so that adds to the price, especially of the perishables."

Atim's face screwed and his head pulled back. "What do you mean 'purse-ibles?'"

"Perishables! Things that go bad. They have to be shipped in more often and some need refrigerator trucks. Adds to the cost."

Chickadee pursed her lips. "And that's also why very little is fresh. Most of the food comes in frozen boxes." She waved at the aisle of frozen platters, pastas, pizzas, and peas.

Otter shook his head. "Grandpa said that stuff will kill you. He says that's why there's so many Elders missing legs. I'm glad he always eats bush food."

Sam looked up from the floor for a second. "Diabetes. That's why there's so many missing legs."

They all nodded.

Atim put his hands on his hips. "People need to eat. With those prices, I bet a lot of people eat bush food."

After a moment, Otter lifted a finger. "Speaking of diabetes, Auntie wants chocolate!"

The other Muskrats giggled and began to make their way to the candy display, which was up at the front where the cashier could keep an eye on it. They waved at the woman behind the register and turned to look at the selection.

Atim shook his head, groggily. "Sometimes, I imagine I've hidden in the store and then at night I come out and eat all the junk food and chips."

Sam grabbed the specific items their auntie had insisted they buy, just as the bell over the Co-op's outside door rang. Everyone looked up to see who it was.

Through the wall of pop bottles, the sound of loosely tied snow boots, hitting the floor in an uneven gait, sounded familiar. *Galunk-gunk, galunk-gunk.*

Otter leaned toward the others and whispered, "Fish."

Fish was a member of Windy Lake. An old boating injury caused him to limp on one leg and slouch forward slightly. His real name was Moriah, which he insisted was from the Bible. But along Windy Lake a moriah was an ugly fish. Most people called him Fish, but they added *ugly* when they were being mean.

It was well known that a lot of the fights and crimes in town were committed by only a few people, and a number of those people were Fish's brothers and cousins. The corner of town where Fish and his cousins lived had become a tough neighborhood. The Muskrats tried to avoid it.

The cashier momentarily froze when the local man rounded the corner. Then she gathered herself and called, "Mel! Deadbeat!"

Fish was more than slightly disheveled and wasn't wearing a winter coat, but rather layers of thinner garments that hopefully added up to warmth. He seemed unfazed by the cashier's concern and gave her a friendly wave as he entered the store.

She repeatedly pressed a button under the counter and shook her head. "No, you don't, Fish. You better get out of here! Mel is coming." She then continued to yell, "Meeeelll! Deadbeat, Mel!"

In short order, the sound of heavy footsteps approached from the rear of the store.

"Who is it?!" Mel's growl came from deep within his T-shirt. While cashiers came and went like leaves, Mel had been the smiling, growling manager of the Co-op for as long as the Muskrats could remember. He was a large and muscled man. An ancient, gray toque tightly hugged his head.

"Fish!" Mel grabbed the much smaller man's shoulder. "Do you have the money to pay your tab?"

Fish shook his head, his eyes filled with pleading. "No, Mel. But I'll have it soon! I just need—"

"If you don't clear your tab, I don't care what you need." Mel pushed his unwanted customer toward the door.

Fish stepped back and Mel grabbed him again.

The smaller man struggled half-heartedly to stay. "Mel, please! I just need one more time! My wife is coming to buy groceries later. Please, Mel! Let her put it on the tab and don't tell her we're behind. *Please*, Mel."

Mel continued to nudge him toward the door. "Get out, Fish."

Fish dodged to evade Mel's pushes. "Mel, remember when we were kids? Remember when we were kids out at the lake?" His voice became muffled each time Mel bumped him with his chest. "We're cousins, Mel! Just one more time. My kids need to eat. Please, Mel."

Mel reached out, grabbed Fish by the collar of his outer layer and shook him. The frustration was obvious in Mel's voice. "Those kids don't deserve a deadbeat dad like you." Holding on to Fish, the store manager almost tossed him toward the door but he stopped. He looked at the floor, torn by the decision.

Fish stood motionless, still caught in the bigger man's grasp, not wanting to do anything that might push the decision against himself.

Mel sighed a deep sigh before speaking again. He shook his head, sadly. "I can't, Fish. It's too much, and the bill is too long. This is the community's store, not mine."

"Please, Mel. Please." Fish looked at the floor, ashamed to be asking.

Mel let go of his cousin. "I can't, Fish. Not this time."

The two men stood in silence for a moment.

"You better go tell Crystal before she gets here," Mel said.

Fish suddenly sobbed. He leaned forward and buried his head in the store manager's chest.

Mel blinked sadly as he patted Fish on the back. On the last pat, he took hold of the smaller man's collar again. "Why do you make me do this, Fish?" He gave his cousin one last shove toward the door. "Stop gambling, Fish."

Resigned to his fate, Fish gave an apologetic nod to the store manager and then turned to leave.

Chickadee's face was filled with sorrow. "That was tough to watch."

Sam whispered gravely, "Poor Fish."

CHAPTER 10

Muskrats Divided

"There he is! Big Hat!"

After dropping off the chocolate at the hall, the Muskrats said good-bye to Harold and Denice and began to scan the crowds at the festival for any of their current suspects. It didn't take long for them to notice a large ball of fox fur bobbing through the lines of people.

Atim, being the tallest, noticed Big Hat first. He hissed a warning.

The Muskrats instinctively walked toward the shadow of the nearest wall.

The large, well-dressed man was strolling nonchalantly through the food court area where a handful of food trucks had circled, and a smattering of picnic tables were strewn. He studied a menu, shook his head, then moved to consider a different truck. Eventually, he stopped at one he found suitable and stood to wait in line.

Atim chuckled. "I guess carrying around that big hat makes you hungry."

Sam shook his head at his brother. "Everything makes *you* hungry."

The Muskrats moved around the nearest corner so they could hide behind a utility shed.

"Is he going to eat something?" Chickadee hissed.

Sam laughed. "I'd be surprised if he's waiting in line to rob the food truck."

Chickadee gave Sam a quick rabbit punch in the lower ribs. "I just didn't think a crime kingpin would be eating at a food truck, smart guy."

Otter shook his head. "Kingpin? Really? I just saw him taking money from a bunch of guys. We don't really know if it was crime related."

Sam chuckled again. "He was just taking money from a bunch of guys in the midst of a sporting event."

Atim also smiled at the smallest Muskrat. "Pretty sure betting is illegal."

Chickadee smirked. "I suppose everyone could have just owed him, and they all chose that moment to pay him back."

Otter shrugged. "Maybe Uncle Levi would know more about him."

Sam nodded. "You're right, Otter, we should ask Uncle Levi about Big Hat."

Atim waved a dismissive hand. "He won't tell us nothing."

Sam smiled mischievously. "Yeah, but if we ask him and he doesn't tell us anything, Chickadee will be able to tell us if he's holding something back. Hey, Chickadee?"

Chickadee nodded. "Yeah…I know Uncle Levi pretty good. I can tell when he's keeping a secret."

Otter held out a hand, signaling for his cousins to be silent. "He's got his food!"

Atim leaned around the corner. "What did he get?"

The other Muskrats pulled him back and pushed him to the rear.

Sam scoffed at his brother. "I think we're more concerned with where he is going and who he's going to meet!"

"You, maybe." Atim was unapologetic as he stood on his tiptoes, to watch as Big Hat took a seat at a picnic table.

Chickadee shaded her eyes with a mittened hand to cut the glare. "Who is that sitting at the other end of the table?"

Sam also covered his eyes as he looked. "I can't see who it is. He's facing the other way. But he's not friends with Big Hat. He didn't even ask to sit down."

The figure at the other end of the picnic table was wearing a green hoody under a gray, quilted work jacket—the kind favored by the local fisherman. From behind, it looked like he was eating too.

Atim squinted as he spoke, "I think...it's a deluxe burger. You can see the two patties...and I think it's fries but it could be a small onion rings."

Otter smacked his forehead, and looked skyward, exasperated by his cousin's ability to focus on the wrong priority. The other Muskrats groaned and shook their heads.

Turning back to their quarry, Sam was surprised to see the man had left. He elbowed his brother in the ribs. "Hey, look! He's gone."

"He left his garbage!" Chickadee muttered, as she peeked around the corner.

Sam shook his head. "Don't worry about that. Keep your eye on Big Hat."

"Yeah. It's fries for sure. Look at the way he's holding them." Atim smiled at the other Muskrats, happy that his mini-investigation had come to a successful conclusion. "I thought maybe it was rings, and we were just seeing the edges. But we'd have seen the whole circle by now."

The other sleuths closed their eyes, counted to ten slowly, and continued watching the man in the big fox hat.

Chickadee hissed. "He's moving over!"

Big Hat slid along the bench on his side of the picnic table. He was now sitting across from the garbage left by the person in the hoody. He started to root through the stuff on the tray.

Atim adjusted his toque. "Ketchup, probably. The red food truck's fries are way better than the ones he got."

After tossing aside the wrapping from the abandoned meal, the man in the big hat revealed a squarish block. He snatched it off the tray and weighed its heft in his hand. All the Muskrats could see was that it was a small, rectangular package, wrapped in a plastic bread bag. Big Hat smiled, and the package disappeared into a pocket of his coat.

Otter's voice betrayed his surprise. "What was that?"

Sam's eyes were big. "It looked like a covert handoff."

Chickadee blinked in surprise. "The guy in the hoody left something for Big Hat hidden in the trash on his tray!"

Sam smacked his forehead. "One of us should have followed that guy!"

Otter had continued to watch the man at the table. "Now Big Hat is taking off!"

Atim stuck his head around the corner to take a quick peek. "It looks like...yep, looks like he's leaving, like, half a burger and three-quarters of the fries."

Chickadee stood and spoke to Atim directly. "That's not what is wrong with this picture!"

Atim turned to her and threw up his arms. "Well, yeah. They left all their garbage on the table too."

Otter continued to keep his eye on their quarry.

Sam stood. Annoyed, he poked Atim on the chest. "Big Hat just left. You and Chickadee follow him and see if he gives that package to someone else. Don't get too close. Otter and I will trail Green Hoody."

Chickadee grabbed the elbow of Atim's snowsuit and began pulling him away. "Let's go, big guy."

"What's his problem?" Atim looked over his shoulder at Sam, who was heading after Green Hoody.

Chickadee scanned the crowd as she hauled him off. "Keep an eye on Big Hat. I'll explain where you went wrong...."

The mystery man's face was concealed in the depths of his green hood, but he was obviously a First Nation man with long hair that hung down his chest. Now, he was wearing his green hoody on the outside with numerous layers underneath. The man's jeans were baggy and ill-fitting. While his face was hidden, the Muskrats soon recognized a familiar limp.

Sam's whisper was filled with surprise. "Is that Fish?"

"Mm-hmm." Otter nodded. "He wasn't wearing the hoody on the outside before. He switched layers, looks like."

Sam pinched his chin. "I wonder why?"

Otter shrugged. "Feeling guilty about something?"

Sam nodded, thoughtfully. "He sure looks at his phone lots."

Sam followed Otter along the edge of the forest as they both looked toward the center of the fairgrounds. Bush-wise Otter walked easily through the underbrush while Samuel stumbled along behind.

Fish meandered through the fairgrounds, seemingly doing nothing but killing time. He wandered between the outdoor trade booths that displayed everything from chainsaws to bulldozers. Every so often, he looked at his phone.

Otter stopped when they had a good view of the row Fish was walking down. "He must be waiting to meet with somebody."

Sam shook his head, stifling a yawn. "He seems to be pretty interested in those snowmobiles."

Their target had stopped in front of a squad of snow-sleds on display. He was engaged in a conversation with a salesperson wearing a green snowsuit covered in patches that advertised a range of products.

Otter sat down in the snow beside Sam at the edge of the bush. Only a short distance away, a refrigerated semi-truck trailer sat at the end of the row of trade goods, humming loudly and keeping the festival's food supplies frozen. Farther down, dozens of people milled about the trade booths, but Fish was easy to pick out.

"That sounds like…. Otter, look!" Sam dropped low to the ground, hiding behind a ridge of snow, underbrush, and dead grass. Otter followed quickly once he saw what his cousin was pointing out.

Fish approached the end of the row, looking at his watch as he walked. He looked over his shoulder, then stood by the refrigerator truck, effectively hiding himself from the festival crowd behind him. He studied his phone, occasionally glancing around.

Sam whispered, "Do you think he's waiting for someone?"

"Looks like," Otter murmured back.

The boys looked at each other. "Could it be?"

It was. In short order, Eddie approached the refrigerated trailer from the center of the festival grounds. He looked around furtively as he approached the meeting place. Thankfully, the ridge of snow hid the Muskrats from anyone approaching from that direction.

Fish adjusted his hood to hide most of his features. He tensed at the sight of Eddie but waited warily.

Once he noticed Fish, the local thug greeted him angrily.

The two boys struggled to hear what they were saying.

Fish was obviously afraid. He flinched each time the bigger man moved. Leaning back, he handed over an envelope, much like the one he had already left for Big Hat.

Eddie looked inside, shook his head, and then swore at Fish. Suddenly, his thick arm grabbed the smaller man and threw him up against the semi-trailer.

Fish spoke quickly, but whatever he said, it earned him a punch to the lower ribs. After a second one, he fell to his knees.

With his foot, Eddie roughly shoved his victim. Fish landed on his side and curled into a ball.

Eddie waved a couple of fingers and screamed, "Two days! You have two days to get me my money!" With that, he left Fish lying in the snow beside the trailer.

The Muskrats raised their heads.

Otter's face was filled with concern. "Should we help him?"

Sam considered, but then his brow furrowed. "Nooo.... We probably don't want either of them to know we saw their little altercation. Fish won't be happy that we saw him go down. Eddie doesn't like us, period." He lip-pointed back down the way they had come. "Let's head down there a little way and then come back as if we just came around the corner of that lane farther down."

Otter nodded. The boys moved as quietly as possible along the edge of the bush, occasionally looking back to see if Fish was paying attention. He wasn't. He was still in the process of lifting himself off the ground. The boys ran out of the bush and alongside the nearest building that marked the perimeter of the fairgrounds. They then turned and began to walk toward the injured man.

By now, Fish was kneeling, his bad leg and the pain in

his ribs making it difficult to rise. He had yet to notice the boys approaching.

Sam called out, cheerful, but concerned. "Hey, you okay, Fish? Can we help?"

Fish turned his head, startled. "What? Oh, Muskrats. Yeah, I slipped. I could use someone to lean on for a second. You know—this darn leg."

The boys helped the bruised man rise. He was only in his thirties, but poverty and the effects of the boating accident made him seem a lot older. Once standing, Fish took a big breath to fully reinflate. He then let it out in a long sigh that dripped with sadness.

Otter's brow furrowed with concern. "You okay, Mr. Fish?"

The man chuckled and patted Otter on the arm before he started limping away. A few steps later, he muttered over his shoulder, "Don't gamble, boys. It isn't good for you."

CHAPTER 11

Clump of Cousins

"You wouldn't believe who it was!" Atim waved his hands wildly to emphasize the incredible nature of their find.

The Muskrats had just finished family Sunday dinner at an auntie's house. She had served it early, so everyone could get to Jeff's flour packing contest on time. Anticipation turned to mounting excitement as the meal disappeared and the sun dipped lower in the sky.

After dinner, the pre-teens and younger teenagers gathered in one of the larger bedrooms to let their food digest before bundling up for the contest. As they regaled each other with tales of bravado and daring, most of the cousins lounged on the two twin beds pushed to either side of the small room. Some perched on a couple of fold-out camping chairs, two sat atop a beat-up dresser, the rest leaned along what little wall space was left over. Now, they were listening to the Muskrats outline their newest case.

Chickadee threw a pillow at Atim, who was sitting on the opposite bed. "Just tell him!"

Atim shook his head and smirked. "No way. He's got to guess."

Otter was the only Muskrat who did not know who the man in the big fox hat had met. Atim had told his brother, Sam, earlier.

"Was it one of the miners?" Otter ventured.

Atim chuckled and shook his head.

"Was it that weirdo who makes the bone jewelry?"

Atim laughed louder.

"How about the creepy guy from the gas station?"

All the cousins chuckled. Atim shook his head.

Sam rolled his eyes at his brother. "Tell him more of the story. You've got to give him some clues."

Atim shrugged. "After Chickadee and I left you guys, we wandered around to find Big Hat. And then, we did. So, we followed him to the parking lot, and we watched him get into a truck."

Otter's forehead scrunched as he pondered. "Whose truck was it?"

Atim shook his head. "If I tell you that, you'll know who it was."

Otter waved a hand at Atim. "You probably don't even know whose it was."

Atim scoffed. "Of course, I do. It was Lars Hammet's!"

Otter's eyes got big. "Lars Hammet? He's come in second for the last three years in the International!"

Atim closed his eyes and clenched his fist to his face. "Duh!"

"If Lars Hammet is in cahoots with Big Hat, that could for sure be motivation for meatball madness!" Sam said.

Atim sighed. "Not Lars! He's such a cool guy."

Otter raised a finger. "Just because he talked to Big Hat, doesn't make him a suspect. We haven't proven anything yet."

Sam nodded. "If there is one thing Otter and I have proven, it's that today was a bad day for Fish."

Chickadee and Atim both looked shocked. "What?"

Sam related the story of Eddie's assault on Fish. "Yeah. It looked like Fish owed Eddie money."

Chickadee's eyebrows rose higher as the story unfolded.

Atim slapped his forehead. "So, Fish owed money to Big Hat *and* Eddie?"

Otter nodded. "And he has run out his welcome and tab at the Co-op too."

Chickadee's shoulders fell. "And it's all because of gambling."

Sam cringed. "I feel bad for Fish, but we have to get back to the case...and Grandpa's task. I'm thinking that Chet is probably our best suspect, if we could kill two—"

Suddenly, the bedroom door swung open. "Hey, you

munchkins! What are you doing? It's almost time to go!" Denice slipped through the doorway, followed by Harold, who was pushing Jody's wheelchair.

Chickadee bounced off the bed and gave her favorite, older cousin a hug. "We're just talking about our newest case." She told Denice what she and Atim had seen earlier in the day.

"So, who is this Big Hat guy?" Denice asked.

The Muskrats shrugged.

Sam pinched his chin as he spoke. "He was taking bets on Jeff's flour packing race."

Denice looked at her younger cousins. "You know, word out of the Drama Station is that Eddie is hooked up with a gang."

One of the local gas stations was affectionately called the Drama Station in recognition of its place in the town's gossip circles.

Sam threw his hand up in the air. "Well, that certainly takes things up a notch!!"

"Eddie has friends in a city gang," Harold told them. "If he's anything like them, he'll turn Windy Lake into his own private crime zone to pay his gang dues."

Otter's brow was furrowed. "I guess it makes sense, then, that Eddie would be taking bets."

Denice nodded. "If Eddie is working for a gang, he's got to pay his dues...any way he can."

Chickadee spoke up next. "Mr. Penner said, whenever there is money involved, especially illegally earned money, there are always shenanigans."

Harold scoffed. "Take it from me. I've lived in the city, and there is no honor—or trust—among thieves."

Otter shifted his hat as he spoke. "We should probably tell all this to Uncle Levi, so at least he knows about Big Hat and Eddie taking bets."

The other Muskrats nodded in agreement.

Denice hooked a thumb over her shoulder. "He's in the garage with the rest of the old men. Go talk to him but hurry up. It's almost time to go."

As the Muskrats left the room, Jody wheeled himself out closing the door behind him. He gave Atim's arm a little tap. "Hey, big guy, can we talk? I just wanted to say I'm sorry for getting mad at you about Muskwa."

All four Muskrats stopped as Atim smiled a little and waited to hear more.

Jody sighed. "I was upset at myself because I wasn't in the race. I took it out on you."

The tallest of the young sleuths also sighed, his smile growing larger. "I love Muskwa. I wouldn't do anything to hurt him."

Jody smirked and slapped the plaster cast sticking out from under the blanket on his lap. "And I should know anything can happen on the trail." His smirk disappeared and a sad look crossed his features. Jody shifted in his wheelchair and paused for a moment before his hands went to his face, as he tried to stifle a sob.

The Muskrats gathered around him. When he noticed the concern in everyone's eyes, he shook his head. "You know…I didn't tell the whole truth about my sled accident."

A gasp went up in the hallway.

With more than a little chagrin, Jody told the Muskrats that he had been training for the adult dogsled race, when a snowmobile came up from behind.

His dogs were used to snowmobiles, but this one came up fast, and right behind the sled. The snowmobile driver slammed into them from behind, cutting Jody's left leg out from under him. Zooming past the dogs, he forced them off the trail. They were in heavy bush, with the team at a dead run, and Jody held on as the sled slapped against the tree trunks. They careered through the unpacked snow.

Jody was in tears when he finished the story. "When the dogs finally stopped, my leg was broke. I couldn't put any weight on it. Now…it may need pins put in."

Sam said quietly, so as not to be too challenging, "It could have been an accident. Came around the corner too fast—didn't see you."

Jody shook his head. "As I lay in the snow, the dogs came back to see what was wrong with me, tangling up the lines, like dummies. But after I got them off, I could hear a snowmobile, idling in the bush. I yelled for help.

Maybe they didn't hear me, but I could hear their engine, so I thought they should hear me. Anyway, they took off."

Otter moved closer to Jody. "Why didn't you tell us earlier?"

"Because...I didn't know for sure that it was intentional. I still don't know, but with all this other stuff, what if...?"

Sam gave Jody a questioning look. "Do you think it might have been Eddie or Big Hat?"

Jody shrugged. "I don't know. I really don't remember much more about what happened. I guess that's why I haven't told anybody. Everyone just assumed the dogs got away from me. No one asked why."

"Give it time, the details may still come to you," Atim said.

Chickadee smiled. "Grandpa would tell you to dream about it."

Atim patted Jody on the shoulder. "Thanks for telling us. And thanks for letting me race your dogs. It was one of the best days of my life...until Muskwa got sick."

Jody smiled. "It's easy to get hooked on mushing behind a team of dogs. I can't wait until this is off so I can do it again."

With that, Jody said good-bye and made his way back into the bedroom.

The Muskrats stood without saying a word for a second.

Sam broke the silence. "Should we ask Harold about the Animal Army?"

Otter nodded, then went back in the bedroom and tugged on Harold's sleeve. When he got his older cousin's attention, he nodded his head toward the door. "Hey, cousin. Can we ask you something where it's quiet?"

Harold followed Otter out of the room. He smiled once he was surrounded by the sleuths. "What do you nerds want?"

Otter giggled. "We were wondering if you've seen those Animal Army people that have been going around town."

Harold shook his head. "No. I have heard them screaming their heads off though," he said.

Atim flicked the hair out of his eyes. "No doubt. They tend to yell a lot."

"Well, a lot of them are wearing hoodies from your university," Otter said.

Harold waved his hand in the air. "*My* university? Let me guess. You Muskrats want to meet them. What did they do, steal rez dogs?"

Otter's eyes got big. "Not yet!"

Sam spoke up, "They may be involved in our most recent case."

Chickadee sighed. "And even if they aren't, Grandpa wants us to find out more about them."

Harold chuckled. "One of Grandpa's little assignments? He's been giving those out since long before you Muskrats came along. All right. I'll track them down, see if I recognize any of them. If I do, we'll set something up."

After the Muskrats thanked Harold, he rejoined Denice and the other cousins.

The sleuths would have to battle a number of challenges to get through the house to their uncles in the garage.

The first was the unofficial day care—the living room.

The unfortunate teen cousins, sentenced to wrangling stampeding toddlers, perked up when they saw the Muskrats. But their spirits slumped when Atim, Sam, Chickadee, and Otter pried the clinging youngsters off of each other and scooted out of the room.

The second challenge was slipping through the kitchen without being overloaded with auntie errands. Although, they tried their best, Atim and Otter had to throw themselves into a request lobbed from the dining table. The two boys were sent outside to the trapping shed to cut off a slice of moose haunch for a family guest who was about to leave.

By moving quickly behind Atim and Otter, and not making eye contact, Chickadee and Samuel made it through the kitchen. They crossed the utility room in a rush. And then, they were sliding through the door to the garage.

The eyes of all their uncles turned. A thick silence fell. Then....

"Muskrats!" The word burst from Uncle Jacob.

The other uncles laughed lightly.

Chickadee beamed. "Hi, Uncles!" She pinched Sam in the ribs, signaling for him to speak.

Sam shook his head and then focused on his band constable uncle. "Uncle Levi!"

Uncle Levi nodded his chin toward Sam. "Mm-hmm?"

Samuel motioned with his head. "Can we see you in the utility room? We need to ask you something."

Uncle Jacob bellowed, "Must be a big case!" He then smiled mischievously. "Now, they need the *biggest* Muskrat." All his brothers, except for Uncle Levi, chuckled.

Chickadee smiled and waved at her uncles. "Bye-bye, Uncles."

The two young detectives and the local police officer slipped into the other room.

Uncle Levi hitched up his belt as he watched his niece and nephew out of the corner of his eye. While the police officer often appreciated the help of the young detectives, their investigations had sometimes been a source of consternation and irritation.

Samuel and Chickadee gave a rushed summary of what they had seen during the flour packing contest, the rivalry between Eddie and Big Hat, and the ominous conversation they had heard in the Co-op. When they were finished spilling the beans, the two Muskrats were gasping for breath.

Uncle Levi pondered. "We'll have to get the RCMP in on this. Quick! Tell me everything. I need details."

CHAPTER 12

Double Bust

"When will it happen?!" Samuel hissed as his foot tapped, incessantly.

The Muskrats were back in an excited crowd watching the flour packing race.

Although it was still a timed event, the final was set up to have the contestants do their "runs" at the same time. Two trucks filled with sacks of flour were surrounded by enthusiastic attendees of the Windy Lake Trappers Festival.

The Muskrats' cousin Jeff, and his rival, shuddered as they inched their way toward the finish line. Both were almost hidden under the mass of canvas sacks filled with heavy powdered wheat.

From his perch atop the tallest Muskrat, Otter scanned the floodlit area. "I don't see any of them!"

Chickadee tugged his sleeve. "How about Big Hat or Eddie?"

Otter looked down at his cousin. "Oh, yeah. There's, like, a three-guy lineup in front of each of them."

Atim was eager to see action. "I wonder when Uncle Levi and the RCMP are going to step in?"

Sam gave his brother a harsh look. "Hey! Not so loud! You'll tip off the gangsters!"

Atim cringed and gave his brother a smile of chagrin. "Just want to see the bad guys caught, that's all."

Sam's eyes got big. He put a finger to his lips. "Then be quiet. It's like hunting. Silence is golden." Impatiently, he ran his fingers through his short hair.

Otter had picked out Big Hat and Eddie earlier. The two stood on either side of the crowd, like two poles of greed and selfishness. The pace at which they were taking bets increased as soon as the emotion of the race heated up.

The Muskrats knew they were the only ones aware something bigger than the race could happen momentarily—and it was important to keep that to themselves.

Sam stood on his tiptoes to scan the crowd.

Chickadee elbowed him in the ribs. "Watch the race. It'll happen when it happens."

Sam rubbed the spot where his cousin made contact. "You sharpen those things?"

Chickadee's eyes narrowed and she cocked her elbow again.

Sam laughed and held up his hands. "Okay. Okay! I'll be *here*. Be *now*. I'll focus on the race."

Each contestant held onto the strap that crossed their forehead and disappeared into the layers of flour sacks. Cousin Jeff was two steps behind, which didn't seem like much, but when each man carried the weight of a small car on his back, it was a lot. Tonight, the contestants started out with the heaviest weight carried the night before—plus another forty pounds. It was a grueling load. Jeff was again in his favorite clothes. His legs shook mightily, but his pace was steady.

The other flour packer was a big man from out of town, who worked at the mine. The arms of his jacket were emblazoned with logos from the mining company and its suppliers. He had managed to take a few quick steps at the start, so he was currently in the lead, but the exertion was turning his face a fiery crimson.

Otter waved his hands in the air. "I think his head is going to explode!"

From below, Atim hollered, "Run! Run! Run!" But a quick shuffle was all the contestants could manage.

Chickadee and Sam screamed as they pumped their fists in the air. "Go Jeff-y! Go Jeff-y!"

The mass of flour piled onto Jeff's shoulders gave him the appearance of a small, roving shed. It seemed to take immense concentration for him to move one foot a few inches forward, followed by the other. His legs quaked.

The other man's effort was just as intense. The veins on his forehead stood out like little red worms.

Otter looked back at Big Hat and then over at Eddie. With their friend in the lead, other miners seemed to be betting heavily. Eddie was still dressed in his big, puffy jacket that looked like it was made from quilted garbage bags. Big Hat was dressed in clothes that Otter thought of as "church clothes," too nice to wear every day. A big cigar burned in his clenched lips and smoke curled up and around his fur hat.

Suddenly, a quarter of the distance short of the finish line, the big miner stopped. For a moment, he wavered, then he took a half-step back.

Sam could see him put all his effort into getting that back leg moving forward again.

Cousin Jeff had now made up most of the difference between them, with his slow and steady pace. His next tortured step had them neck and neck, with just six feet left to go.

The big miner leaned forward. He tipped his load's momentum forward and got moving again. The two contestants mirrored each other's slow, tiny steps. It looked like it was going to be a tie.

Having leaned forward to get moving, the momentum within the big miner's load was due to roll back. When it did, the big man was pulled to a stop, just for an instant. It was enough.

Jeff had a toehold on the lead. With pained steps, he crossed the finish line mere moments before his opponent.

The Muskrats went wild, jumping up and down.

After the packs of flour were carefully unloaded from the contestants, the crowd rushed in to congratulate them both. The Muskrats ran to Jeff once he was safely out from under the massive weight.

The crowd surrounding them was just as jubilant. Of course, those who had bet against Jeff were not so happy. But tonight's event was going to be the talk of the town, at least until the start of the Windy Lake International Sled Dog Race.

Chickadee grabbed Jeff's hand and looked up at her big cousin. His happy face was framed by his shoulder-length black hair, and it held a huge smile. Tears of joy rimmed his eyes. "I did it! I won!" Jeff looked around at his little cousins.

All the Muskrats gave him a big hug. They let go as the organizers called the two flour packers up on the nearby stage. With the awards for first and second place given out, Cousin Jeff held his winning trophy aloft, proudly waving it in the crisp night air.

The police moved in as the crowd began to thin.

Big Hat was still counting his money when the four RCMP officers approached him with their guns pointed at the ground. They quickly surrounded the well-dressed gangster. The city man shook his head, smiled, and lifted up his hands, still holding fans of cash. The officers walked Big Hat, uncuffed, back to their car.

On the west side, Uncle Levi and Gus approached Eddie with their guns still in their holsters. The two RCMP along with them had their guns drawn and targeted.

They approached the local hood from the rear. His head was down, nothing was in his hands, but he had a backpack slung over one shoulder as he walked away from the stage.

Approaching from behind, an RCMP officer kicked Eddie's legs out from under him. With a crunch, he landed on his stomach. The officer leapt on Eddie's back.

Eddie cursed loudly, trying to roll over. This caused the second officer to join in, rip the backpack off Eddie's shoulder, and toss it a few feet away. The two Mounties roughly snapped on a set of handcuffs as they berated Eddie and lifted him to his feet.

Uncle Levi and Gus frowned, shaking their heads, hands on hips. They were obviously disappointed in how the RCMP carried out the arrest. They watched the two Mounties haul their suspect off to their cruiser.

The Muskrats ran up to their uncle talking excitedly.

His frown disappeared and quickly switched to laughter as he raised his arms in surrender. "It's done, Muskrats! With your help, we've caught the bad guys. The Windy

Lake International Sled Dog Race and the Trappers Festival are safe."

The leftovers from the crowd had stopped to gawk at the police officers around them. The speaker system crackled to life, and the announcer assured everyone that the excitement was over. He asked the crowd at the Windy Lake Trappers Festival to applaud the RCMP and the Windy Lake Band Police. Then the announcer said, "I've just been told…this is another case that was solved with the help of the Mighty Muskrats!"

A crackling of applause could be heard across the festival grounds and on the speaker system. After that, Atim, Chickadee, Otter, and Sam couldn't walk anywhere without someone coming up and shaking their hands. However, Uncle Levi warned them not to speak about the details of the case, so the Muskrats moved on when someone pressed for particulars.

"Hey, you kids! What are you doing?" Harold tried to disguise his voice, but he was giggling by the time he finished speaking. "Congrats on doing whatever you did."

"Thanks!" Sam smiled. "It all happened pretty quick."

Atim proudly stuck out his chest. "Never would have happened if I hadn't lost the youth race."

The rest of the Muskrats rolled their eyes.

Harold shook his head and chuckled. "Everyone is talking about it."

Otter blushed and looked at his feet. "We just wanted to make sure the adult sled dog race was fair, that's all."

Harold gave Otter a friendly push on the shoulder. "Well…I got something that you all wanted."

Sam's eyebrow shot up. "Really, what is it?"

Harold snickered. "It's a date with a nice girl."

Atim's eyes got big. "A real date?"

Harold laughed. "Hold your horses, Romeo. I ran into that Animal Army of yours. When they were off duty, I guess."

A smile grew on Chickadee's face. "Really? So, did you know any of them?"

Harold nodded. "Yeah, a girl who was in a law course I took. We had to do an assignment together with a couple of other people. Her name is Millie."

"Will she meet us?" Sam asked. "Grandpa wanted us to find out more about them."

Harold rubbed Sam on top of his toque. "Just solved one case and you're already looking for new adventures, hey?"

Sam used his forearm to push back his older cousin's hand. He squinted at Harold and straightened his cropped top. "No need to muss the hair."

Harold guffawed. "All right, Muskrats. It's been a long day, so I got to go. But Millie said she would meet us tomorrow. Show up at the Station at lunchtime."

"We'll see you there!" Atim shouted. He was standing behind his brother and waiting for Sam to finish straightening his hair. Just as Sam was about to put on his toque, Atim reached over and playfully messed his hair up again.

CHAPTER 13

Colliding Perspectives

Dramatically, with one knee hitting the dirty restaurant floor, Otter sang along with Nazareth on the jukebox as the Muskrats entered the Windy Lake gas station.

The other Muskrats burst into laughter. A few people at nearby tables did too. But not the waitress assigned to seat them. She waited with her hand on her hip.

Sam smiled up at her. "We're supposed to be meeting our cousin Harold here."

The teenager shrugged an apathetic shoulder and pointed with the end of her pen around the room. "I don't see him, do you?"

Sam took a slow look around the square room. "No."

The server put her hand on the stacked menus. "So? Are you guys actually going to order something? Do you have any money?"

The young sleuths all nodded.

The waitress took an extra slow blink, then began counting out the laminated food lists. "How many?"

Sam scrunched up his face, waggled a hand, and squeaked out, "Six...maybe?"

The server rolled her eyes. She dropped the menus on the table and announced over her retreating shoulder, "I'll be back in a minute to take your drink order. Be ready."

Atim looked after her as she left. "She'll be a great leader, one day."

Harold and the girl from the Animal Army showed up soon after the waitress left.

The Muskrats recognized Millie immediately as the girl from the Co-op. She had been told the Muskrats wanted to meet her, but not why. She arrived full of curiosity, which only grew when she recognized the Muskrats as the kids from the altercation at the Station. Her parka and sweater were comfortable and fashionable, but not as flashy as some of the other university students' winter clothes. Her heart seemed to smile when her face did.

"Hey! You're the kids from the trapper's truck." Millie pointed at them with a painted fingernail.

Atim's eyes got big. "Oh, boy."

Chickadee nodded, making an effort to maintain a neutral face; she had yet to decide if she liked this young woman.

Sam cringed a bit, then smiled. "Yeeaahh. That's what we wanted to talk to you about."

To the Muskrats' surprise, Millie apologized as she pulled out a chair. "Well, I'm sorry for that. It was stupid. Chet is a bit of cowboy. He goes overboard sometimes." She shook her head. "Most times, if I'm honest. A bunch of us almost left."

Otter closed his eyes, remembering back to when the Animal Army surrounded Uncle Jacob and his catch of furs. When he opened them, he looked seriously at Millie. "That really freaked us out."

She shrugged. "Like I said, I'm sorry. It all happened in the heat of the moment. You know…," Millie looked down at her fingers, "…I have always wanted to see a mink. And when I finally did, it was hanging from a string in that trapper's hand. Made me sad for a second, then mad."

Chickadee blurted out, "He's our Uncle Jacob. He gives a lot of what he catches to the Elders for food."

"I'm a vegetarian."

Atim chuckled. "Our family chases down moose and eats them raw." His smile disappeared when he saw how Millie reacted to his joke.

Harold had also taken a seat. He waved at the tallest Muskrat. "Down, boy."

Sam changed the subject. "Our Grandpa gives us assignments every once in a while. We told him about what happened, and he wanted us to find out more about how you and your friends think."

Millie asked, "How we think?"

Chickadee squinted as she spoke. "I think, he wanted us to know more about you."

Millie smiled. "I guess, there are a lot of different parts to me. There's the Chinese me, there's the Canadian me. My parents moved from Hong Kong when I was just a toddler. Since then, we've lived in two Canadian cities. And…we never left the cities. I can't remember if I ever saw a farm or a small town when I was a child."

Sam pinched his chin as he tried to explain. "What part of you is in the Animal Army? Our Grandpa says that you might see animals as humanity's cousins too, just like we do. So, he thinks you're maybe more like us than other city people."

Millie lowered her head in thought. When she spoke, it was quietly. "I don't know about that. I think your uncle should consider what those animals went through. The pain each one felt." Her face twisted with the thought.

Chickadee almost stood up. "Uncle Jacob tries to be as gentle as he can when he harvests animals. He hates to see them suffer."

Millie's face twisted with annoyance. "But he kills them!"

Chickadee shot back. "Everything dies. At least he's not like *your* people. City people kill everything that gets in their way. Not just in ones and twos but in large numbers."

Millie shook her head like she was trying to dodge a bee. "What? I don't kill anything!"

Chickadee said, "If you support the city, you support killing thousands of animals and plants."

Millie turned her head and looked out the window. "I don't know what you're talking about."

Harold looked concerned. "Hey, let's not let this get out of hand."

Otter spoke softly, "If we expect Millie to tell us about her perspective, maybe we should share ours first?"

The other boys nodded.

Chickadee took a deep breath. "Yes. Sorry. We shouldn't expect you to give us a gift if we have not shared a gift with you first. That's what my Grandpa would say, anyway."

The university student pursed her lips, then let out a long breath. "I want to understand. I'm willing to listen."

Sam looked at his cousins. "Where do I start?"

Otter smirked and lifted a shoulder. "Maybe start where Grandpa would start."

Atim raised his eyebrows and threw up his hands in faux anger. "That far back? We'll be here all day!"

Everyone laughed, which helped to relieve the tension.

The waitress came by and took everyone's drink order.

When she was gone, Sam scratched the back of his head as he collected his thoughts. "Well, my grandpa would say, 'You are the land you live on.' And that means, when people live on a landscape, they have to get their food and shelter and water, and everything else they need to survive through the seasons of that land. Repeating that, year after year, creates a lifestyle. After that lifestyle is lived through a few generations, people start to have stories of ancestors who carried out the same tasks or who defended their lifestyle. That's when it becomes a culture. And when those people reach for the stars, and the stars reach down, that desire to understand something bigger becomes their spiritual beliefs."

Millie leaned on the table, listening intently. "Well, that's super interesting, but how does that relate to my being a vegetarian?"

Atim snapped his fingers, then leaned back in his chair. "A guy's got to eat. And around here, if our ancestors had tried to be vegetarians, they wouldn't have made it through a single winter."

Samuel straightened and pointed at the roof. "Yes. That's what I was trying to get to. What my brother says is true. We are the land our ancestors lived on…and that we still live on. The growing season is too short to grow crops around here. Our main food sources were moose and wild rice, because that was what was most plentiful, or provided the most nourishment for energy in the cold."

Millie flicked an arm skyward to emphasize her point. "But you don't have to do that now! You can buy wheat and corn and almonds and even meat, if you must, from the city."

Chickadee harumphed. "But don't you see? Don't you

see how you support the killing of so many just by saying that?"

Millie shook her head. "I don't support that!"

Chickadee crossed her arms. "I think you mean…you let someone else do it for you."

Otter sighed, loudly, then he looked over at Chickadee. "There's so much to explain. Let's try to do it step by step. We want Millie to understand, right?"

Chickadee pursed her lips, then nodded.

"Well, she can't do that if she has her walls up," Otter remarked.

Chickadee sighed but she looked Millie in the eye and apologized to her. Then she turned to Sam. "Go on."

Sam was uncomfortable explaining things to someone older than he was. But then he considered that it was his Elder who gave him the task. "I think what Chickadee is talking about is how city people farm. You know, they kill hundreds of species of plants just to fill the field with one crop, like wheat. They also chase away or kill all the animals who will eat the grass their cows need to eat. And they'll kill all the predators in an area, just to make sure their cows and sheep and chickens are safe."

Millie looked shocked. "But I don't…."

Chickadee's eyebrow shot up. "Eat crops? Your crops mean algae in the lakes, and bees dying…and roads!"

Millie's face darkened. "Roads? What are you talking about? If any animals get killed on the roads, it's by accident."

Atim rubbed his tummy. "Mmm…roadkill. Where's that waitress? I'm starved."

Everyone chuckled and the tension of the last few minutes ebbed again.

Sam smiled. "You seem like a nice person, so I'm sure if you hit an animal with your car, it's an accident and you feel super bad about it."

Millie made a sad face. "I ran over a raccoon once. I tried to stop, but I couldn't. It *was* an accident."

Sam tried to look compassionate but serious. "It may have been an accident to you, but my Grandpa would say it wasn't an accident for your culture."

Millie looked doubtful. "I don't get it."

Otter took off his hat, scratched his head, and then put his hat back on his head. "You know, every day when people wake up and get in their cars, they know that there will be animals killed all over Turtle Island."

Sam nodded. "Yeah, maybe not by them, but someone will accidentally kill an animal for every so many miles of road, every day. Racoons, geese, deer, moose, little birds, even helpful insects, like dragonflies. The drivers will be sad. But as a people, as a culture, and nation everyone accepts that, when they get in their cars, many animals will die because of their moving machines. They just hope it's not their turn to have an…accident."

Atim's faced twisted with exaggerated disgust. "Skunks!

People run over skunks." He pretended to gag. "I hate that smell."

Otter slapped him on the back in an attempt to help.

Millie ignored their antics and replied thoughtfully, "I see what you mean. We just accept that as a 'cost of doing business.'"

Chickadee's tone was once again combative. "Wouldn't be so bad if the business was just your business, but the city people's way of doing business is having an impact on the entire planet."

Millie didn't take the bait. She completely changed the subject, instead. "You know, Chet…. When he gets in people's business, the problem isn't that he's a fanatic. It's that he labels people."

Sam frowned. "You mean, he puts a dollar value on other people?"

Millie shook her head. "Um…no. I mean, once he calls you 'enemy,' according to his rules, he doesn't have to treat you with respect or decency. You're just the enemy from then on. All you have to do is disagree with him a little bit, and you become one hundred percent evil."

Otter winced. "That must be tiring."

Chickadee's eyes got wide. "So, does he really care about the animals?"

Millie raised her palms skyward. "Hard to say. Does he really care? Or does he just want to fight? I don't know. We're all watching to see what he does."

Atim murmured to himself, "Or what he did."

Millie overhead him and frowned. "I do wonder what those boys did during those days before we arrived."

CHAPTER 14

Rainbows R Us

The server showed up and dropped off the drinks. She took everyone's food order, but not before rolling her eyes at the vegetarian's questions about the food.

After the diversion about Chet, Millie had collected her thoughts. "Okay. If you're so worried about roadkill, how do you explain your uncle trapping?"

Harold lifted a hand and waggled it back and forth. "When it comes to that, things have changed since the city people showed up. Now, we kill things because they have value in the city people's economy. But long ago, before the fur trade, we had different reasons for harvesting animals."

Millie pushed her line of thinking. "But I think it is wrong to hurt an animal. Your uncle doesn't seem to think so."

Chickadee sat up straight. "Yes, he does!"

Her cousins all nodded vigorously in agreement.

Sam waved a hand in the air, as if to erase a bad thought, before he tried to explain. "Going back to the beginning…when my uncle kills, let's say, a deer, he will try to do it as quickly and painlessly as possible. He will honor the spirit of that deer, put tobacco down maybe. But then he will honor the Greater Deer Spirit, which that individual deer was a reflection of. And this Greater Deer Spirit can be…offended, if that individual deer is not given the respect it deserves."

Chickadee tapped the table. "If my uncle is cruel, for example."

Millie cocked an eyebrow. "The Greater Deer Spirit isn't offended by pain?"

Atim's voice was serious. "It is natural for a deer to be killed by wolves or hunger or disease. Those all include pain. Considering how long a life can be, a few moments or even days of pain at death is…certainly a possibility."

Otter looked out the window at the forest across the highway as he spoke. "And we're talking like someone is making decisions. But that is *not* it. Grandpa would say it's more like the laws of nature."

Sam looked chagrinned. "Yeah. That's right. You don't decide to be affected by gravity."

Harold slapped him on the shoulder and smiled. "Hey, Muskrat. You're doing fine. Keep going."

Sam shook his head. "This might not be how an Elder would explain it. But I think, it's how I understand it...."

The Muskrats all gave him looks of encouragement.

Millie looked confused.

Harold came to Sam's rescue. "Well...some of this stuff is what we'd call a 'worldview' in university. And for Cree people, a worldview is often covered by sacred stories and ceremony. And there's rules about sacred stories and ceremony."

The girl from the city waved her hand and shook her head. "I don't want anyone to get into trouble."

Otter smiled at her, reassuringly. "I think it'll be okay if he just speaks of his understanding and doesn't act like he is representing the teachings."

Harold agreed.

"Thanks, you guys," Sam said. He looked at Millie. "These are only my words, you know. I just moved out to Windy Lake and heard the stories not that long ago."

Chickadee squeezed Sam's arm. "Maybe that's why you're the best to explain to someone who comes from the city."

Samuel continued on. "It *is* more like nature's laws than a conscious decision. Water flows downhill because of gravity. The Cree don't worship the sun, but we respect it as the source of energy that life is built from."

Millie nodded in understanding. "Okay. Go on."

"So...the Greater Deer Spirit is like a prism, and when

the light of the sun shines through that prism, the spirits of the individual deer are formed. So, it's Father Sky and the sun that pour into the individual deer all those things that aren't bone, flesh, or blood—like personality and instinct and spirit."

The waitress showed up and plopped down the food, not caring about who had requested what. After she left, they all focused on making sure each menu item went to the correct person. Eventually, everyone had their own food, and the chaos settled down.

Millie waved around a fork full of salad as she spoke. "So, you were saying?"

Sam's eyes went wide. "Poop! Where was I at? I forgot."

Otter gave him a nudge. "You were talking about the sun and Father Sky."

Harold made a motion toward Millie with his teacup. "Wait a minute. Millie, do you know anything about the Cree language?"

Millie shook her head.

Harold took a sip of tea. "Well…you know how French splits everything into masculine and feminine?"

Millie nodded. "Yeah. I spent a summer in Quebec when I was a teenager. Almost everything is labeled either male or female."

Harold nodded. "Well, everything in Cree is split into 'that which has spirit' and 'that which does not have spirit.' Or animate and inanimate."

Atim nodded wisely and lifted a finger. "Energy and matter!"

Millie's eyes got big. "Okay. That's cool!"

Harold nodded and smiled at her. "It is cool." He lip-pointed at Sam. "Go on, Samuel. I just wanted to mention that."

Sam gathered his thoughts. "All right. So, the Great Deer Spirit is like a prism that casts all the individual deer spirits onto the earth. And like a prism splits the sun's light, so the Great Deer Spirit creates a rainbow of different traits. Each individual deer has its own...hue, its own special color of the rainbow."

Chickadee smiled at Millie for the first time. "We're like that too. We're each our own special piece of a rainbow, that's why we all have different personalities, talents, and dreams."

Sam scratched the back of his neck. "In a way, there's another rainbow...the rainbow that comes from Mother Earth."

Millie's face skewed in confusion. "You mean...a rainbow of mud?"

All the cousins laughed.

Atim began to tick off his fingers. "Well...you got prairie people, mountain people, desert people, seashore people, island people...volcano people! There's lots of different Indigenous cultures."

Sam grinned at his brother. "He's talking about what

we said before…the teaching that you are the land you live on. There are different lessons of Creation from the different landscapes. And when people live on those landscapes over time, they create different cultures."

Chickadee brought her hands together lightly. "So, you have the coming together of two rainbows. Even before you are born…you are what your mother eats, and she eats what comes from the land."

Millie nodded, a growing understanding inside her. "But what about city people?"

The Muskrats and Harold looked at each other.

Otter smirked and shook his head. "That Grandpa! I think he wanted *us* to figure this stuff out, instead of *you*."

Harold slapped the table. "That sounds about right."

Everyone chuckled.

Millie looked around the group. "Well then, what about city people? Does 'you are the land you live on' apply to them?"

"Of course!" Sam said. "It's a landscape too. But…."

"But what…?" Mille wanted to know.

"Well, it *is* a landscape, but it is manmade. So, Grandpa says it is *created*, as compared to being something that was a *part* of Creation." Sam's smile was slightly embarrassed.

Atim waved a hand. "When Grandpa gets ranty, he says there's no such thing as a self-made man in the city, and that Canadian culture will never be Indigenous because its base is cows and wheat."

Millie giggled. "What is *that* supposed to mean?"

Sam gave Atim a slight punch in the arm. "What my brother is trying to say is, the city culture in North America originally came from the Fertile Crescent in the Middle East. That city culture may have altered somewhat as it gained new technology and was influenced by different lands, but it has always brought along its cows and wheat."

Otter shook his head. "And concrete!" he added.

"If there was a city culture born in Windy Lake, I bet it would be based on delicious moose meat and wonderful wild rice," Sam speculated.

"Moooooose!" Atim howled at the roof. Everyone in the restaurant turned to look.

Otter laughed. "And berries!"

Millie shook her head. "Cows and wheat, I never thought of that!" She tapped her lips. "My people's culture didn't start in the Fertile Crescent, but we still clear out diversity to plant our crops and raise our domesticated birds and livestock. It even seems it's easy for people from different city cultures to do well when they move to each other's cities; there are a lot of common teachings. But... tell me. What is something that is different between city cultures and Indigenous cultures caused by the landscape of the city?"

All the Muskrats and Harold were silent for a moment as they pondered the question.

Chickadee started off, thoughtfully. "Well…Grandpa says that our families are the building blocks of our nations. But in the city…."

"…it's all about the individual." Millie pointed at Chickadee.

Harold playfully grabbed her finger. "'You are the land you live on' even trickles down to etiquette. We don't point."

Millie pulled her finger away. "So, what do you do?"

Everyone else at the table lip-pointed at her, and then they all broke out in hysterics. After eating and more discussion, the Muskrats said good-bye to their older cousin and their new friend. Understanding had been shared.

CHAPTER 15

Case Ajar

"Hey! Ms. Chick-a-dee-dee-dee-dee!"

The Muskrats had left the gas station restaurant after finishing their lunch. In the parking lot outside, Dave—otherwise known as Pop Guy—was unloading goods for the convenience store. The large Canadian man made his voice as high pitched as it would go to sing out the last dee-dee-dees. His huge size indicated he had unloaded a lot of trucks.

"Hi, Pop Guy!" Chickadee smiled at the frequent but short-term visitor to Windy Lake.

Pop Guy's route usually brought him around every second day for as long as it took to remove the Station's order from his delivery truck and put it on the shelves.

He lifted a big box and stacked it atop a couple of others already on the dolly. "I asked for that information you wanted. Got a lot of weird looks."

Sam and Otter looked at Chickadee with two more weird looks.

Dave pointed at them. "Yeah! Looks just like those."

Chickadee smacked her forehead. "I forgot I asked!" When the Muskrats had bumped into him at the Co-op, Chickadee asked him for a favor, but then it slipped her mind in all the excitement. "What did you find out?"

Dave loaded another box on the dolly as he spoke. "Well, I asked all the stores on my route. In Slateville and Smokey Bend, the clerks all mentioned they saw a guy come in and buy up most of their hamburger. He hit both stores on the same day, so he must have done a bunch of driving. Give me a minute." Dave kicked the bottom of the dolly forward, so it rested on its wheels. He began to whistle as he pushed the load of store goods into the Station.

After he was gone, Samuel looked at Chickadee and raised an eyebrow.

Chickadee shrugged. "We always say, you need flour to make bannock. I figured, you need meat to make meat-balls. The Co-op rarely has more than a couple packs of hamburger at any time. And when we saw Dave…."

"Great idea!" Sam gave Chickadee a high five. Atim and Otter patted her on the back.

The fringe over Atim's eyes danced as he shook his head. "I thought we solved the case."

Sam pinched his chin as he thought. "Maybe, we just

solved the case of the greedy gamblers. Let's hear if Dave has a description of the guy."

The bell over the Station door tinkled as Dave pushed his dolly back out and toward his truck.

Chickadee skipped over him. "Thanks for asking around for me, Pop Guy."

Dave chuckled. "I've been doing this route for so long, but you Muskrats are the most interesting thing to come down the pike in a while."

Sam smiled at the delivery man. "That's nice to hear. Did the store clerks have anything more to say?"

Dave leaned on the top of the dolly as he thought. "In Smokey Bend he just bought hamburger. But in Slateville, he bought...what did you call them, Chickadee? Carsick pills?"

Chickadee nodded at him.

"Yeah, well, Slateville has the biggest store," Dave continued. "The clerk there said she remembered him because he bought a lot of a weird combo—raw meat and tummy pills."

Atim smirked. "For me, one often leads to the other."

Pop Guy Dave snorted a quick chuckle.

Sam raised a finger. "They didn't happen to say what the guy looked like, did they?"

Dave pointed at Sam. "Focused. I like that." He leaned his head back in thought. "Well, they both said the same thing. The guy was wearing a hunting jacket—camouflage, they said. Native guy, long black hair. Oh! And he had a limp. Both said he was slow-moving…he had one beat up leg. Not a new injury, but an old one. One of the ladies said she was worried about the guy. Said he looked frail and could hardly carry his load of heavy meat."

The Muskrats shared a look amongst themselves.

Otter whispered, "Sounds like Fish!"

The delivery man smiled at the detectives' reactions. "Did I help with something?"

Chickadee leaned over and gave Dave a pat on the arm. "You did, Pop Guy. You may have saved the Windy Lake International Sled Dog Race!"

Dave was impressed. "Really?"

The Muskrats all nodded. The tallest Muskrat held up his hand to give Dave a high five. The huge man returned it with gusto.

Atim winced at the impact. He shook the sting out of his hand as he spoke. "Could we pay you back by helping you unload your truck?"

The delivery man's face broke out in a smile. Dave thanked the young sleuths, then directed them to get into the back of the huge truck and move the boxes closer to its rear, so he could then roll them into the store. When all of the groceries were shelved, Dave loaded up the dolly, said good-bye to his helpers, and continued along his route.

The Muskrats took off to their fort to discuss the latest developments.

"We have to catch Fish!" Sam slammed his fist into his palm.

The Muskrats had gathered in their abandoned school bus. Sam and Otter sat on the beat-up couch, Chickadee was at her computer, and Atim sat on the edge of his weight bench.

Atim looked concerned. "Why can't Uncle Levi go get him now? We know he bought the hamburger."

Otter shook his head. "We made facts where there are no facts!"

Chickadee's face grew stern. "What do you mean, Otter? Big Hat and Eddie were doing bad stuff."

Otter's lips tightened. He let out a big breath. "But look! Now, we have to catch Fish, with less time before the start of the race. We just took it as a given the race rigging was connected to Big Hat and Eddie. Then we got new 'facts.' Looks like Big Hat and Eddie could be bad, but so could Fish—possibly. We have to *prove* that his hamburger was actually the meatball hamburger."

Samuel nodded. When he spoke, his voice was dripping with disappointment. "You're right, Otter. We *assumed* that Big Hat or Eddie made the meatballs. We didn't turn it into a solid thing. We still haven't solved the Case of the Rigged Race."

Atim threw up his hands. "Are we back at square one?"

Sam stared at his shoes, thinking. "No. We can't assume, but we *can* focus on Fish for a while. Find out more. We could be at square one, but we also have a strong suspect."

Otter let out a big sigh, happy he didn't have to do any more convincing. "So, what do we have to do?"

Chickadee smacked the side of her computer. "We need more info. You can't make bannock without flour. I wish this thing could help!"

"What we need is eyes. We need to see Fish with the meatballs," Sam said.

Atim shook his head. "So, we have to catch him as he is trying to fix the race? Shouldn't we try to stop him before that?"

Sam gave his brother a funny look. "Well, seeing him throw the meatballs during the teen race would be evidence, but that's already over. What do you suggest we do?"

The Muskrats sat in silence as a wave of tension ebbed.

Suddenly, Chickadee smacked her computer and whooped. The boys jumped.

She grinned at them. "The Trappers Festival has a video and photo contest this year, right? Like last year?"

Atim yowled. "Yeah! #WindyLakeFurFest!"

Sam laughed. "Of course! We just need to look for videos and pictures online!"

Otter pointed at the old, yellowed computer that his

cousin used. "Get that thing going, Chickadee. Let's look at what people put up."

The Muskrats' computer whizzed reluctantly. Chickadee patted the aged monitor lovingly. "This ol' girl? When have we watched video on her?"

Sam waved a hand at the old machine. "Let her sleep. I bet Mr. Penner would let us use the computers in the science lab."

The other sleuths cheered in agreement.

CHAPTER 16

Hashtag Hassles

The Muskrats were just entering Windy Lake when they heard a truck coming up behind them. A red Ford slowed to a stop beside the young gumshoes. It was an old truck and the smoke from its exhaust warmed the local climate.

The passenger's side window opened, and a First Nation woman stuck her head out. "Hey, you Muskrats! My husband wants to talk to you."

Otter's eyes got big. "Is that Fish's wife?"

Chickadee nodded, slightly worried.

Their cousin Denice had been high school friends with Fish's wife, so she had been invited to family events back when the Mighty Muskrats were younger. Fish's wife, Crystal, was from a much better family, and much to their consternation, she had fallen in love with him back in high school.

Seeing that his cousins and younger brother were

reluctant, Atim stepped toward the truck. The darkness inside meant he could not see anything beyond the woman and her tattooed arm. "What can we do for you?"

Crystal shook her head at him. "Not you. Those two." She pointed at Otter and Sam.

After a shared glance, "those two" stepped a small step forward.

"Come on! I'm not going to bite you!" The woman waved them closer and then laughed with someone inside the vehicle.

Atim followed the other boys closer.

Once they were a step away from the truck, they could see through to the shadowed interior.

Fish leaned on the driver's wheel, an unexpected smiled beamed from his face. "I wanted to thank you kids for helping me the other day. Not too many people are good to me in Windy Lake. Could be because of my family, I don't know. But you Muskrats helped me when I was down."

Fish's wife tapped the door of the vehicle. "You kids ever need anything to solve one of your cases or something, you let us know. We owe you a favor."

Suddenly, Sam blurted out, "We're looking for hamburger!"

The woman laughed. "Hamburger is expensive in Windy Lake, and there's always only a little bit." She flung a thumb at her partner. "This guy was craving a burger so bad the other day, he went all the way to Smokey Bend to get some ground meat. And then he forgot the buns."

The three boys watched Fish, whose smile had disappeared.

Sam squinted, trying to see their suspect better. "We found some meatballs that had some drugs in them. Our Uncle Levi sent them for DNA testing, so he can match it with any other hamburger found in Windy Lake."

Mrs. Fish scowled. "That's weird. Why would someone do that?"

Fish's eyes almost popped out of his head. "Well, heck!" His voice quivered as he put the truck in gear. "We have to hit the road, just wanted to say thanks for the help the other day. We got to go…."

With that, he hit the gas and sped away. His one tire chirped as it gained traction on the pavement. The Muskrats were left in a cloud of snow.

Chickadee let out a breath. She had not inhaled the whole time Fish had been close. Then they all looked at Otter.

He shook his head. "Fish freaking out and booming off is not evidence yet. Maybe he really was craving a burger. We have to get proof at the computer lab."

The Mighty Muskrats broke into a jog. The school was almost on the other side of Windy Lake. As they skipped, hopped, and loped past the arena, the young detectives caught sight of Denice and Harold unloading boxes from an auntie's van. Like four banshees, the Muskrats ran up shouting greetings. Their older cousins shook their heads but smiled a welcome at the younger family members.

Harold smirked. "Now, we're in trouble."

After almost toppling her over with a hug, Chickadee beamed up at Denice.

Atim, Otter, and Sam began to help unload the boxes onto a four-wheeled trolly beside the van.

Sam smiled at Denice. "We just ran into Fish. You were friends with his wife back in high school, weren't you? Talk to her lately?"

Denice chuckled. "Yeah, Crystal says they've been down on hard times. Fish can only do odd jobs here and there. He's got his issues, that guy. She says her biggest problem these days is keeping Fish from gambling all their money away."

The Muskrats shared a look.

Harold gave Samuel a little punch in the arm. "You blew Millie's mind, little cousin."

Sam scratched the back of his head through his toque. "What do you mean?"

"You cracked her egg!" Harold laughed. "She got so fired up, she went back to her friends at the Animal Army and caused a rebellion. She convinced a bunch of them they weren't doing the right thing here. The rebels headed back to the city."

The Mighty Muskrats beamed bright smiles.

"Really? She changed her mind?"

Harold snickered. "You inspired her, I guess. She was talking crazy. Said she was going to start the Urban Horse Initiative, or something like that. She said that car culture is killing the planet, and the horse brought mankind to the twentieth century *without* causing climate change. She figured cities should have strategies in place, in case they suddenly have to switch back to horses."

Otter lifted a shoulder. "I'm for the idea!"

Chickadee clapped her hands. "Me too. That's so cool!"

With quick good-byes, the Muskrats resumed their jog toward the school.

Windy Lake Elementary had put in a lot of good years and they showed. On the edge of the big lake, its schoolyard ended with a tall fence that kept students from reaching the water. A half-century of wet and winter winds off the lake had eroded its edges, worn its wood, and smoothed its stucco.

The Muskrats hit the doors of the school at a run. Closing in on the science lab, Atim called out, "Mr. Penner! We need to use a computer to save the Windy Lake Trappers Festival!"

Mr. Penner was at his desk in the science lab and had obviously heard Atim because he greeted them as they arrived. "The game is afoot!"

Atim frowned. "No, Sir! It's meatballs, remember? I

don't know what we'd do if we found a foot!" He looked wide-eyed at his cousins.

Sam shook his head at his brother. "Read a book, Sherlock."

Chickadee lip-pointed toward the door that led to the computer lab. "Mr. Penner, can we use the lab? We need to look at a lot of videos and our Wi-Fi isn't good for that."

Interested, Mr. Penner removed his reading glasses, and held them in his hand as he spoke. "What are you checking out? Did the pills lead to further clues?"

Chickadee nodded. "I found the website you mentioned. We figured out the pills were Dramamine."

Mr. Penner pursed his lips, seriously. "The test shows you're right. Remember, I took a sample when you were here last time? Well, I got the results back. It was cow meat and it did contain some form of Dramamine."

Atim whistled low.

Sam's eyebrow rose. "That makes it official then."

Otter scratched his head. "We still don't know if they're Fish's meat."

Mr. Penner shook his head. "They aren't. The test shows they are cow."

The Muskrats giggled.

Sam smiled. "Sorry, Mr. Penner. We have a suspect. His name is Fish."

Chickadee tapped the science lab table. "That's why we need to use the computers. My old clunker has terrible

Wi-Fi, and we need to have more eyes on the project than one screen can handle."

Mr. Penner smoothed his mustache as he spoke. "Well, good! Obviously, you're on to the next challenge."

Otter's brow furrowed. "Like Chickadee said, we need eyes, Mr. Penner. Lots of them."

Sam explained. "We need to check out as many images from the photo contest of the teen race as we can to see if someone was throwing the meatballs on the trail."

As the Muskrats started on their way to the computer lab, Mr. Penner made a face, considering the situation. "I was surprised at how many entries there were when I looked at the hashtag earlier today. That may be a lot of bush to cut through."

He was right.

The Muskrats had gathered around Chickadee's screen. After she had pulled up the site, she threw her hands in the air. "There's way too many!"

Standing behind her, Sam squeezed her shoulder. "Don't worry. We'll all look."

Chickadee's voice betrayed her frustration. "Yeah. Well, how are we going to divide them up? Where do we start?"

Otter squinted an eye. "We found the meatballs by the Cedar Point viewing area. I think we could start there."

Sam nodded. "That's the *where*. We need another of the Five Ws."

Atim pointed at his brother. "We could look at the times just before the race."

Sam waggled his head back and forth. "The race volunteers would probably be checking the trail before the race. If I was Fish, I'd do it after the trail had been checked."

Otter shrugged. "Now, we got a *where* and a *when*."

Sam smiled, as he pulled out the chair in front of the computer next to Chickadee's. "Let's get to it!"

Atim started at the next one over. "I bet I find it!"

Chickadee scoffed in his direction. "Yeah, right! My machine is humming! I've already watched one video!"

Racing to find their next clue, the Mighty Muskrats waded into the hundreds of clips using the hashtag: #WindyLakeFurFest.

After thirty minutes, Chickadee sighed. "A lot of these don't have time stamps!"

Otter held up a hand. "I think I found Fish!"

The other sleuths clustered around him.

Atim slapped Otter on the back. "That's him!"

Sam pushed his face past his cousin to get a better look at the paused video. "Where is he?"

They all moved in until the screen's glow tinged their faces.

Chickadee almost touched the screen with a finger, gesturing to a corner of a building in the upper section of the shot. "He's still at the festival grounds. He's carrying a bag of something."

"Before or after the race?" Atim scowled.

Otter gestured to a few spots on the screen. "See those shadows? They'll point away from the direction of the sun."

Sam pinched his chin. "And…the sun is in the same general area, time, and place each day as it crosses the sky."

Otter grinned and nodded. "So, we should be able to figure out the time of day by figuring out where the sun was by looking at the shadows. That's the back of the festival gift shop, isn't it?"

"Yes!" Chickadee smiled.

Sam squinted at the bit of building in the frame. "Yeah. You can see where the sidewalk is for the public washrooms."

Otter stood upright and closed his eyes. "What time was sundown yesterday?"

Sam squinted as he thought. "Just before five o'clock-ish, I think. It's winter, gets dark early."

The most bush-wise of the Muskrats used one finger to trace a line in the air where the wall would be. In his mind's eye, he imagined being on that exact spot, the small gathering hall and gift shop in front of him, a crushed limestone parking lot beneath his feet. With his other finger, he imagined he was moving the sun back and forth in the sky. Due to its being a priority of his grandparents' teachings, Otter had a good idea where the sun had come up that winter morning and where it would sink behind

Mother Earth. When the shadows matched what he saw on the screen, he guessed a time of day based on the position of the sun. "About an hour or so *before* lunch, I'd say."

Atim slapped Otter on the back.

His cousin grinned, thankful his skill was appreciated and trusted.

Sam slammed his fist into his palm. "We have to speed this up. The race is tomorrow!"

Chickadee nodded. "I'm going to do a search for *Fish* and *Cedar Point*. And then, if we match those two up, we might find the right time."

The others agreed and went back to work.

Sam grabbed the hair on either side of his head. "We have to hurry! And…there's…so…much…stuff!"

Atim held up a hand. "I got a Fish. No time stamp."

Otter went over to see. "That's *before* the race. See the shadow from that tree?"

A few minutes after that, Chickadee squealed. "I have a good one. This one is by someone who works at Cedar Point. Shows them arriving at that viewing spot. I'm going to go through the rest of her stuff."

A silence settled in, broken only by mouse clicks and the whir of little fans.

A few minutes later, Fish was found. He was behind some people who had gathered to cheer on their favorite racer. The time stamp was forty minutes before the race started.

Atim flicked his head to get the hair out of his eyes. "He would have to drive to Cedar Point, right? This would give him time to drive there, and then with his limp, get to the viewing area."

Sam grinned at his brother. "Good thinking! We really need to find him, in that place, at that time."

Chickadee rubbed her eyes. "I can't take much more of speeding through video. I think I'm getting motion sickness."

Otter snorted. "Too bad Uncle Levi took what's left of the Dramamine meatballs."

They all laughed. But the smiles faded as fast as they went back to their screens.

Time was ticking.

"What's that!" Chickadee stood quickly and pointed. The boys gathered around her.

The video was taken within the crowd at the Cedar Point Viewing Area. It was shaky and showed the tops of the trees and the sky more often than people. Chickadee paused it. A sea of arms and cut-off heads lined the bottom. Bush and a stretch of blue lined the top. She pointed out a forearm and hand in the back that seemed to be in the middle of an arc and pressed play. The hand rose and disappeared behind the crowd. It looked like it was in mid-toss, but the launch point was hidden behind other arms.

Atim snapped his fingers. "You know, there's a picnic table back there. I saw it sitting empty in another video."

Otter pursed his lips. "Fish was sitting down in that earlier video. He probably sits when he can because of his leg."

Sam lifted his index finger and made a circle in the air. "Let's round up video clips that show that picnic table if we can."

They all got back to work.

It was another twenty minutes before Sam howled. "This is it! You got to see this!"

The others gathered around his screen.

Where Sam started the video, the person holding the phone had it aimed at a team coming around the corner and going down the trail. As the dogs passed, the cameraman continued to pan into the crowd and down to his wife and two small children standing near the edge of the crowd.

"How do you like the dogsled race?" he asked the two small girls in their snowsuits. Their blonde curls bounced as they nodded enthusiastically.

Chickadee giggled. "Ever cute."

The young spectators' mom smiled brightly as she kneeled between them and hugged them close. Sam paused the moment. "Okay, watch here." He pointed to the waists of people milling about in the background of the family scene and pressed play.

As the family scene continued in the foreground the people behind them watched the race and wandered about. Suddenly, a break in the flow allowed a square of the sky to be seen between the trees. Below that, Fish was pushing himself off the picnic table. The crowd began to react as another team came near, but the camera continued to focus on the family. For a few seconds, the crowd closed, and Fish was hidden.

Chickadee gasped, disappointed.

But then Fish reappeared, and he had something in his hand. He hefted it, feeling its weight, and then he threw it. In the foreground, the family still bantered. Sam rewound the video to the point Fish was judging the weight of his projectile. Sam paused the video. Hovering in the air above Fish's hand was a dark ball, consistent with the size of the meatballs they had found in front of the Cedar Point Viewing Area shortly after Atim lost the race!

"I think we have our evidence," Otter said in a hushed voice.

His cousins nodded solemnly. It was time to tell Uncle Levi everything they knew. Without another word, the four sleuths turned off the machines, left the computer lab, and went to find their uncle.

CHAPTER 17

Capped Off

Uncle Jacob's truck slid to a stop in a cloud of snow dust.

"Get in!" His rough voice demanded action and the Muskrats hopped into the truck without hesitation.

"Where are we going?"

The Muskrats were all curious. They had been walking down Windy Lake's main road to the arena to help their aunties. Now they were sinking into their uncle's truck seats as he rapidly accelerated.

Jody leaned over the back of the front seat. "The Swamp." He chuckled and rolled his eyes.

The Swamp was a low-lying part of the reserve that always felt damp. Cattails grew in odd places. With most of it unsuitable for houses, it formed a large part of the Windy Lake trailer park neighborhood. It had a reputation as a part of town where bad things sometimes happened.

The sleuths could see in the rearview mirror that Uncle Jacob's brow was furrowed. "Your Uncle Levi called me and told me to get down to the Swamp. When I asked him where, he told me to listen for the dogs."

Jody smiled back at his younger cousins. "Muskwa and his girlfriend got off their leashes the other day. We haven't seen them since. I figure Uncle Levi is trying to break up a dog fight."

Wide-eyed, the Muskrats took in the information.

In a few minutes, the truck was sliding to another stop, a cloud of flying snow engulfing the vehicle before it floated away. A few police vehicles were already there, lights flashing against the sparkly snow. It seemed every dog in Windy Lake was there too.

"Wow!"

"Would you look at that!"

"What's happening?"

Everyone in the truck was enthralled with the scene. Many of the dogs wore collars, some did not. Mixed in among the stray dogs was someone's sled dog, Old Harry's dog, the Bakers' dog, and a few more, including Muskwa and his girlfriend. A few mutts were taking turns diving into a garbage can. Most were chasing each other around as they competed for big chunks of frozen hamburger. One dog would get a lump, and try to eat, but then another dog would steal it. When that dog tried to eat, a different dog grabbed it. It went on and on, and there were at least five big chunks. It looked like football practice for a canine team.

The RCMP and band officers stepped onto the field as the opposing team, trying to grab hamburger balls so they could control the dogs. In the middle of it all, Fish was sitting on the ground, his wife shaking her finger at him.

Uncle Jacob opened his car door and swung out. "You Muskrats help me round up our dogs."

Happily, the four young detectives piled out of the truck, and each ran to grab a furry friend.

Atim chased after Muskwa, who wasn't going to be caught until he was ready. Chickadee took a more strategic course, calling Muskwa's girlfriend whenever the dog wasn't chasing a lump of hamburger. She smiled at Chickadee but took off when a meatball came close.

Sam had grabbed the collar of a passing sled dog and hollered as he was effortlessly dragged across the snow-covered lawn.

A large mutt had caught hold of Otter's hat, and it was now facing the smallest Muskrat, bowed low to the ground, and challenging Otter to a game of Grab the Hat. When Otter stepped forward, the sled dog took off, its smile muffled by the toque in its teeth.

Eventually, the police got hold of most of the big chunks of beef, broke them up and fed them to the dogs. Once the meat was gone, the canines were much easier to catch.

The Muskrats helped their uncle get his dogs into their own little cabins in the back of their truck. The other mutts, strays, and collared dogs dispersed to look for the next bounty provided by Windy Lake and its surroundings.

With the dogs gone, everyone turned their attention to Fish. He sat in a heap with Crystal standing over him.

As he stepped forward with the other band officers, Uncle Levi gave the Muskrats a little wave that told them to stay back until it was safe. Once Fish was surrounded, Samuel signaled the others to follow.

Uncle Levi leaned toward Fish. "That was a lot of meat, Fish. You okay?"

The thin man threw up his hands. "They took it all!" he sobbed.

The band officer took off his hat, scratched his head, and then put it back on again. "Dogs will do that. They like meat."

"Not the dogs!" Fish waved an arm and hung his head. "Those blood-sucking bookies, Eddie and that city slicker with the cigar. They took my family's money!"

Crystal smacked the back of his head, but her voice was sad when she spoke. "Fish…what did you do?"

"They took it all!" Tears streamed down his face now. "Eddie took most of it." He looked up at Crystal. "Eddie took most of it."

Uncle Levi reached down and put a hand under Fish's

arm. He lifted up the much smaller man so they stood side by side. With his other hand, Uncle Levi brushed off the sticky snow from Fish's pants.

Fish looked at his wife. "Eddie won't take my bets anymore." His shoulders tensed and he clenched his fist in front of his face. "He cut me off! I had no chance to win my money back."

"*Our* money, Fish?" His wife's voice held a touch of pleading, a symptom of her hope.

He shook his head, sadly. "Eddie cut me off, so I went to the man from the city, Eddie's competition, but I lost there too. He took what was left."

Uncle Levi shifted his weight. It was time to reveal what the Muskrats had told him. "Why'd you try to drug the sled dogs, Fish? Why the hamburger?"

"I couldn't even bet on the youth race! I knew everyone in it, I knew who was going to win. But they wouldn't let me bet." Once again, he lifted his fist to his face, his voice quivered with emotion. "I wanted to get back at them. I wanted to get back at them both."

Fish's wife collapsed into the snow. Crying, she reached out and held on to his pantleg. "Why, Fish? You told me you won your bet on the flour race. Where…where did you get the money for the meat and gas?"

Fish sank to the ground beside Crystal and spoke through gritted teeth. "I had to get them. I had to get them."

By this time, the couple's many children had gathered around. From teens to toddlers, they all watched the sad scene.

Crystal pleaded, "What did you do, Fish? What did you do?"

He shook his head. "I knew if I messed up the odds, they could lose a lot of money. I could break their game, and then *they* would lose. They would lose all *their* money. If I couldn't win, there was no way I would let them win." He looked directly into her eyes and whispered, "So I took the Christmas money...."

Crystal let out a noise that was both bawl and growl. Two of the younger daughters came forward and put their arms around their parents. A teenager squeezed her mother's shoulder.

As Fish pulled himself from the embrace, their girls rushed in to fill Crystal's arms. Kneeling in the snow, he eventually looked at the band constable. "I had to see if the drug would work. That's why I did what I did."

Uncle Levi pursed his lips. "Revenge?"

Fish closed his eyes. When he opened them, he looked down at his wife and their daughters in their group hug. With a sob, he called to his other children, still standing in a circle. The family came together in their disappointment and sorrow.

Uncle Levi leaned over them. "You know, I have to talk to you down at the station, Fish."

Fish looked up, tears in his eyes, he nodded, then buried his face in his wife's shoulder.

Uncle Levi patted Fish on the back. "I'll be back in an hour or so, Fish. We'll go for a chat."

Later that evening, the Mighty Muskrats were sitting around their grandfather's fireplace with their uncles, Levi and Jacob, and the patriarch of the family. Hot beverages warmed cold hands.

"You should have seen all the dogs!" Uncle Jacob slapped his knee. "That crazy Fish, he got scared after you spoke to him on the highway about drugged meat."

Uncle Levi raised an eyebrow. "Whose idea was it to do that?"

With a touch of hesitation, Sam raised his hand.

Uncle Levi shook his head. "You wanted to see how he'd react when you said it?"

All the Muskrats nodded.

Grandpa chuckled. "But you gave it away!"

Their band constable uncle nodded. "Got to be more careful with those words. If Fish was smarter, he might have hidden the evidence better! You're lucky."

Sam's mouth opened to stammer out an apology, but his uncle waved a hand at him. "Don't worry about it, I might have done the same thing."

Samuel ran his fingers through his short hair and gave a grateful nod to his uncle.

Atim wiggled in his chair. "Come on, Uncle Levi. What about Fish?"

Uncle Levi winced a little before he spoke. "Like I said, Fish isn't too smart. He must still have had a bunch of hamburger in his freezer. But after smarty pants here…," Uncle Levi gestured at Sam and smiled to let everyone know he was joking, "…spilled the beans, Fish got scared, abandoned his plan, I guess, and threw away all the hamburger. So, by the time we got there…."

Uncle Levi began to laugh again. "Those dogs…."

Uncle Jacob slapped his brother on the back with a big whack. "Get it together and tell the story. You're a grown man giggling like a little kid."

Uncle Levi coughed, and his laughter slowed to a chuckle. "Okay." He snorted. "After everyone left, I think, Fish's wife switched from sad to mad. When I returned to pick him up, he was pretty happy to be taken away."

Everyone snickered. Atim nodded at his uncle. "So, this time we saved the race?"

Uncle Levi scratched the back of his neck. "Well…yes. If Fish had carried out his plan for vengeance and thrown drugged meatballs into the adult race, and if that had ended up making dogs sick, then a lot of people would distrust the race, and the organizers, for a long time."

Uncle Jacob harrumphed. "Would have looked bad for Windy Lake, that's for sure."

Sam pinched his chin. "Would he have got his revenge?"

Uncle Jacob shook his head. "Hard to aim a meatball. If you want to take out a specific team, how do you make sure the right dogs get it? It would be even harder if the teams were all bunched up."

The uncles nodded.

"But if all he wanted to do was mess up the race so the bookies' odds were off, then yeah. He could have made Eddie and the city guy lose big," Uncle Levi said.

Chickadee shook her head.

Samuel had a smile on his face. "I think we've finally resolved the Case of the Rigged Race."

Uncle Jacob shook his head. "What about those crazy city kids?"

Uncle Levi shrugged. "Meh. They've obviously done this activism thing before. Now, the Animal Army asks us where to stand when they want to make noise. Turns out, that Chet guy is fairly law-abiding, especially now, with three-quarters of his soldiers jumping ship."

Grandpa looked over at his grandchildren. "From the story Chickadee told me, it sounds like you had quite the impact, Sam."

Sam blushed red, speechless.

Grandpa reached over and patted him on the shoulder. "Now, I hope you can all see the power of understanding."

The Muskrats nodded.

Uncle Levi looked at his watch. "We've got to go."

The young detectives were surprised by the sudden change in their usually slow-moving uncle.

Uncle Jacob and Grandpa also rose. It seemed the Muskrats were the only ones not in on the plan.

Otter raised an eyebrow. "Grandpa, the Windy Lake International doesn't start for a while. We could hang out a bit more."

Grandpa waved the Muskrats toward the trucks. "Come on, Muskrats. We've got to go in a little earlier. Got stuff to do."

The young sleuths didn't question any further. Atim and Otter jumped into Uncle Jacob's truck. Sam and Chickadee hopped into Uncle Levi's. It didn't take long for them all to arrive at the fairgrounds of the Windy Lake Trappers Festival for the start of the big race.

The preliminary events had been going on for a while, and there was a large crowd in front of the main stage. The emcee's voice boomed from the stage as he told well-worn jokes usually reserved for the summer powwow.

Off to one side, Chet's Animal Army had shrunk to a lethargic squad. Penned in by a snow fence, the activists still made sure their voices were heard as they waved their signs at the passing crowd.

At the side of the stage area, Uncle Levi raised his hand in the air.

The Muskrats giggled as their usually controlled uncle gestured and hopped frantically, hoping to get the attention of the emcee speaking from the podium.

When the man finally saw their uncle, he stopped what he was saying and asked the Windy Lake Chief and Council to come to the stage. As the Muskrats tried to walk past their Uncle Levi, he held out an arm and stopped them. "Wait."

Once the town's VIPs were on stage, the announcer introduced the Chief, who came up to the microphone and looked over at the Mighty Muskrats. The Chief was wearing her headdress and the beaded vest she always wore to special occasions.

"For those of you from out of town, you might not know the young people I'm about to introduce. But for those from Windy Lake, I have no doubt you already know them." She gestured for the Muskrats to come over and up the stairs leading to the stage.

Uncle Levi pushed the Muskrats forward. "Go on. This is for you."

Chickadee looked back at her Grandpa. He smiled at her, nodded, and then lip-pointed to the stage, urging her to step forward.

The crowd had created a pathway for the young sleuths.

Atim tried to smooth his hair. "Is this really happening?"

Sam slapped him on the back. "It is, big brother. Don't trip on the steps on the way up."

Atim's eyes got big. He looked at the steps, suddenly, aware of the size of his feet.

Chickadee chuckled. "Don't get freaked out."

Otter, the shiest of them all, walked past the other Muskrats. His voice trembled a little as he spoke. "Come on, we have to keep going." He waved for them to follow.

The other cousins followed Otter.

By the time they were on stage, the Councillors of Windy Lake had joined the Chief. They all watched the young sleuths as they approached. The Chief spoke into the mic again.

"In our tradition, the way to be a good person is to use your talent for the good of your family and community. In our tradition, bravery, honesty, humility, kindness, pride, respect, and self-discipline are not just ways to be polite. They are laws that flow through all of Creation and give a person their integrity. Integrity is important, not just for people, but for competitions too." The Chief went from looking at the crowd to waving the Muskrats to come forward.

Sam noticed that the people from Windy Lake were regarding them with pride.

The Chief arranged all the Muskrats in a line, then went back to the podium. "These young people, the Mighty Muskrats as we call them, have protected the integrity of the Windy Lake International Sled Dog Race, so that when it starts later today, it is something that the people of this territory can be proud of."

A round of applause went up.

Atim leaned over and whispered to his brother, "I think I need to pee."

Sam whispered back, "Don't worry. I'm sure this will be over in an hour or so."

Chickadee chided out of the corner of her mouth, "Stop talking, boneheads. You're ruining the moment."

Grandpa led their family through the crowd to stand directly in front of the stage. The Muskrats' parents, aunties, uncles, cousins, second-cousins, third-cousins, fourth-cousins, family friends, and acquaintances carried bright smiles and proud hearts. Uncle Jacob grinned up at the Muskrats. Beside him, Jody was in his wheelchair, tightly holding on to the leash of an excited Muskwa. Denice and Harold made funny faces at their younger cousins on stage, teasing them for being the center of attention, but obviously proud of them too.

The Chief's voice boomed. "The Mighty Muskrats have used their talents to protect their community and…." The Chief looked over at Uncle Levi.

Uncle Levi stood on the side of the stage, obviously moved by the respect being shown to the young people he and their other Elders had helped mentor. When he realized everyone was waiting for him, he jumped. He blushed red as he quickly walked over and handed four caps to the Councillors.

The Chief started again. "For protecting their community and being young people we can all look up to, the Council and I have passed a band council resolution to make the Mighty Muskrats honorary members of the Windy Lake Police Force!"

The crowd cheered.

The Councillors stepped forward and placed the official baseball caps of the Windy Lake Police onto the heads of the honored detectives. The hats were all too big. They fell down over the Muskrats' eyes and hung at odd angles from their heads.

As a joke, Otter walked around in a small circle, his arms reaching out to find his way. The Councillor behind him laughingly grabbed his shoulders and faced him back to the crowd.

Everyone, including the other Muskrats, had a chuckle.

"Did you want to say a few words, Muskrats?" The Chief stepped aside and held an arm out toward the podium.

Sam stepped forward, his voice betraying his nervousness. "This is a great honor, and we are very proud to be working alongside our Uncle Levi, even if we trip him up sometimes."

A chuckle rippled through the crowd.

Much of Samuel's nervousness disappeared. "And thank you to Chief and Council for this. Windy Lake is great place to grow up!" He reached out to his cousin. "Chickadee, did you want to say something?"

Chickadee paused, but then approached the microphone. "I want to thank my aunties and uncles, and my mom and dad for all they do for us. Without them, we couldn't have done what we did."

Otter quickly stepped forward. "And I want to thank my Grandpa…and my Grandma. I wish she was here. But they taught us everything we know. I wouldn't know how to track, canoe, or tie my shoes without them and all the Elders…."

Atim was wrestling with the butterflies in his stomach, but when it was his turn, he stepped forward one slow step at a time.

Sam covered the mic and whispered to him, "Just say what you feel. You don't have to be deep."

Atim took the mic. He took a deep breath, smiled, and then screamed, "Windy Lake is the best! A big shout-out to all the dogs in the Windy Lake International. Yahoo! Let's get the race started!"

Everyone cheered and waved their arms in the air.

As the Muskrats stepped off the stage, they were met with hugs, smiles, and congratulations from the people they loved.

ABOUT THE AUTHOR

MICHAEL HUTCHINSON is Swampy Cree from the Treaty 5 area and a member of the Misipawistik Cree Nation. During his early years, he fought forest fires, worked in an underground research mine, and did catering for rock concerts and movie shoots. As an adult, he has switched back and forth between the communications and journalism sides of the desk, hosting APTN National News for seven years, co-hosting CTV Morning Live Winnipeg, and working for numerous First Nation advocacy organizations from the national to the local level, including the Assembly of First Nations and the Manitoba Keewatinowi Okimakanak. He is currently the Communications Manager at the Manitoba First Nations Education Resource Centre. He wrote the Mighty Muskrats Mystery Series to educate young Canadians, build pride in First Nation and impoverished youth, and create a better Canadian and First Nations relationship.